The Legend of the Shark Goddess

A Nanea Mystery

by Erin Falligant

★ AmericanGirl®

Published by American Girl Publishing

18 19 20 21 22 23 24 QP 10 9 8 7 6 5 4 3 2 1

All American Girl marks, BeForever™, Nanea™, and Nanea Mitchell™
are trademarks of American Girl.

Cover image by David Roth and Juliana Kolesova
Author photo by Reverie Photography
Grateful acknowledgment is made to the following for permission
to use images in the cover design: "Hawaiian Island Natural Beauty"
©iStock.com/Gary Gray

Cataloging-in-Publication Data available from the Library of Congress

*For my brother, born on Pearl Harbor Day,
and my grandfather, who bravely fought in the war*

Beforever™

The adventurous characters you'll meet in
the BeForever books will spark your curiosity
about the past, inspire you to find your voice
in the present, and excite you about your future.
You'll make friends with these girls as you share
their fun and their challenges. Like you, they are
bright and brave, imaginative and energetic,
creative and kind. Just as you are, they are
discovering what really matters: Helping others.
Being a true friend. Protecting the earth.
Standing up for what's right. Read their stories,
explore their worlds, join their adventures.
Your friendship with them will BeForever.

TABLE *of* CONTENTS

Nanea lives in Hawaii on the island of Oahu, so
you'll see some Hawaiian words in this book.
The meaning and pronunciation of these words
are provided in the glossary on page 208.

Nanea's name is pronounced *nah-NAY-ah*. It
means "delightful and pleasant."

chapter 1

Rules, Rules, Rules

CRASH! NANEA SAT straight up in bed, her
heart racing. Was it a Japanese bomber? Another
attack on her quiet Honolulu neighborhood?

"Mele!" She searched the floor beside the bed
for her dog, who was terrified of loud noises. But
the dark room was empty, lit only by thin cracks
of light around the heavy curtains covering her
windows.

Nanea squinted to read her clock. It was after
seven, so maybe Mom had let Mele outside. But
what had made the loud noise? She held her breath,
listening.

Then Nanea heard a swell of laughter from the
living room—and her older sister's voice. "Rock,
step, left, right. Iris, that's the wrong foot!" As more

1

peals of laughter spilled down the hall, Nanea leaned back against her pillow with relief.

Ever since Mary Lou and her friend Iris had become junior hostesses for the United Service Organization—the USO—they'd been practicing the jitterbug.

But do they have to do it first thing in the morning? thought Nanea.

She threw back the covers and padded into the living room.

"Hey, sis!" Mary Lou was still in pajamas, her dark hair in braids.

"Hi, Nanea!" Iris was in pajamas, too, since she had stayed the night. She flashed a smile before twirling underneath Mary Lou's arm—or trying to. She tripped over a basket of yarn and fell backward onto the sofa, laughing.

"Take a turn with me," said Mary Lou, reaching for Nanea's hands. "You know how to dance the jitterbug."

Nanea yawned. "I don't really," she admitted.

"Yes you do! I've been teaching you. Let's show Iris how it's done." Mary Lou talked through the steps. "Rock back, step forward, left foot, right foot. See?"

The jitterbug felt so choppy compared to hula. Nanea held tight to her sister's hands.

"Quick, quick. Slow, slow," Mary Lou instructed.

Nanea tried to tell her feet what to do. But as Mary Lou pulled her into a twirl, one foot didn't listen. It tripped right over the other.

"It's hard!" Nanea cried, laughing. "You can dance the jitterbug with soldiers. I'm going to stick with hula."

Mary Lou finally let her go. "I'm not choosing one over the other," she said as she pulled Iris back up off the sofa. "I'll never give up hula."

"Good!" said Nanea, feeling a wave of relief.

She and Mary Lou had been taking hula lessons

from *Tutu*, their grandma, for as long as she could remember. Their class regularly performed for soldiers at the USO, but ever since the war began, it was an even bigger deal. "Tutu says our performances are important," she reminded Mary Lou. "They help soldiers forget the war, at least for a little while."

"Being a junior hostess is an important job, too," said Iris, smoothing out her pajama top. "But there sure are a lot of rules to follow, like about how we dress and how we behave."

Mary Lou raised her finger in the air. "Don't forget the most important rule of all."

"No chewing gum?" guessed Nanea.

"No, silly! No dating soldiers we meet at the dance hall."

Nanea cast a sideways glance at her sister. "But what if you meet a soldier as handsome as Al?" She batted her eyelashes.

"Oh, you!" said Mary Lou, swatting her away.

Everyone knew that Mary Lou had a crush on Iris's older brother. But now he was away at war, just like Nanea and Mary Lou's older brother, David. Al had been one of the first people Nanea knew to sign up.

"I wish I'd get a letter from him," said Iris, sinking back onto a pillow. "When we won the Battle of Midway last month, I thought this whole war would end and Al would come home."

But the war hadn't ended, and a day after the battle, David had enlisted. Nanea felt a lump in her throat, remembering. He'd left for Army boot camp just three weeks ago, but it felt more like three years.

"I have to finish my letter to David," she said out loud, reminding herself. "But writing letters is so hard these days!"

Nanea had to think about every word, because her letters would be censored. Someone at the post office would cross out anything that could help

Japan plan another attack on Hawaii.

"I can't even write about the weather," she complained. "Since the war started, there are so many rules, just like at the USO." She started to list them. "Rules about carrying our ID cards and our gas masks everywhere we go."

"Rules about turning out lights and covering our windows during blackouts," said Iris. "Oh, and gasoline rationing! We can't use very much gas because the military needs it."

"Don't forget about curfew," added Mary Lou. "There are rules about when we have to be home at night, too."

"Rules, rules, rules," said Nanea with a sigh. Sometimes it was hard to remember them all.

"Rules are usually made for a reason, girls," said Mom as she stepped into the room. "We don't know everything the government knows about the war. So we have to trust that the rules are there to keep us safe, and then do our best to follow them."

When Nanea saw that her mother was dressed for work, she popped up. "Is it time to go already?"

Mom worked at the Red Cross, teaching first aid and doing other things to help the war effort. Today she was dropping Nanea off at Pono's Market, her grandparents' store, along the way.

"Almost time," said her mother. "Go ahead and get dressed. And don't forget to feed Mele."

Nanea ran to her bedroom—but halted in the doorway. "Oops!" That was Mary Lou's room now.

She backtracked to the room next door, which was David's old room. It was hers now, but she didn't want to change a thing about it. Not the poster of Duke Kahanamoku, David's surfing idol, hanging on the wall above his bed. Not the Boy Scout shirt hanging in the closet, covered in badges. Not David's name tag from the Royal Hawaiian Hotel, where he had worked as a bellhop. And *definitely* not the photo of David and Nanea that was taped to the mirror above the dresser.

No, Nanea wouldn't change a thing. *Not until David comes home,* she vowed.

She got dressed quickly and then attached her special pin to her dress. Papa had given it to her. "Remember Pearl Harbor," the pin read. But instead of the word *pearl,* there was a delicate pearl gem.

Wearing the pin made Nanea feel closer to Papa, especially since he was gone so much. He had been working double shifts as a welder at the Pearl Harbor shipyard, the site of the attack. Nanea was proud of Papa for the important work he was doing. But him being gone was another way the war had changed things for her family, and it was one of the *hardest* changes.

Nanea brushed her hair and took one last look in the mirror. Then she grabbed the canvas bag that held her gas mask and hurried out of the room.

Halfway to the back door, Nanea could already hear the scrabbling of paws.

A-roo!

Nanea's dog, Mele, greeted her happily. But the *poi* dog, a mixed breed, was as smart as she was friendly. She whined as soon as she saw the canvas bag strapped over Nanea's arm.

Many people on Oahu had stopped carrying their gas masks, but Nanea still took hers everywhere. It was the rule, and she wanted to be safe. But the gas mask was a sign to Mele that Nanea was leaving.

A-roo! Mele cried again, as if to say, *Take me, too!*

"I wish I could, silly poi dog," said Nanea, bending down to scratch her behind the ears. "Everyone is always leaving you behind, aren't they?"

Ever since Pearl Harbor had been attacked, Mele seemed afraid to be alone. She had run away from home during the bombing, frightened by the loud noises. And she had been gone for two whole weeks!

Now Mele tried hard to stay by Nanea's side. And that's just where Nanea wanted her, too.

"I won't let anything happen to you," she said, filling Mele's food dish. "But I have to go to Pono's Market. I have a job to do."

Mele barked sharply.

"I know," said Nanea. "*You* have a job to do, too. We'll go to the hospital to visit the soldiers next weekend."

Every week or two, Nanea brought Mele to visit wounded soldiers. Spending time with the friendly dog perked them right up. That's why Nanea called her visits Operation Mele Medicine. One soldier said that seeing Mele was better than any medicine the doctors could give him. Nanea had even taught Mele to dance hula with her, and their act was a hit!

"You have an important job to do, too," Nanea said again. She kissed Mele's scruffy head.

As Nanea followed her mother out the door, she turned to look at the blue star in the front window. That star meant that a family member was away at war. She was so proud of her brother, but she couldn't help thinking of the *other* stars—the gold stars in the windows of homes of soldiers who would never return from war.

Nanea shivered in the early morning breeze. Then she hoisted her canvas bag onto her shoulder and hurried down the steps.

chapter 2

Stolen Goods

AS NANEA PASSED the barrel of oranges, she reached out to tidy the pile of fruit into a perfect pyramid. The new shipment had arrived last night, and she had been there to help Tutu and *Tutu Kane* unpack it. She liked to make each display as pretty as possible for their customers.

"Nanea, do you have the duster?" Tutu called from the next aisle.

Nanea pulled the feather duster from her apron pocket and hurried it over to her grandmother.

"*Mahalo.* Thank you."

As Tutu dusted the lip of a shelf, Nanea took a moment to inspect the rows of canned milk that she had arranged last night. She rotated one can so that the red carnation on its label faced forward, just like the other labels. *Perfect*, Nanea thought.

"You did a good job, *keiki*," said Tutu.

Keiki was the Hawaiian word for "child." But now that Nanea was working at Pono's Market several days a week, she felt more grown up than ever. She was helping her grandparents keep their shelves stocked and their customers happy. That was difficult to do during the war, when shipments of food from the mainland sometimes came late— or didn't come at all.

Tutu Kane said Nanea wasn't quite ready to ring up sales at the cash register yet—not until she had mastered her times tables. So she had been practicing with her flash cards at night.

She studied the jars of guava jelly on the shelf. "There are three rows of jars," she said, counting. "And seven jars in each row. So that makes . . ." She scrunched her eyes shut. "Twenty-one jars!"

Tutu smiled. "Yes. Very good."

Nanea hoped Tutu Kane had heard, too.

Tutu nodded toward the front of the store. "Will you turn the sign and open the door?"

Nanea hopped to her feet. Flipping the sign from "closed" to "open" wasn't as exciting as using the cash register, but it was still an important job. It signaled the start of the shopping day.

As she stepped toward the window, Nanea saw customers waiting with empty shopping bags. When markets in Honolulu received hard-to-get foods, the newspaper advertised the shipments. And people flocked to the stores like hungry birds.

Nanea quickly flipped the "open" sign. As soon as she unlocked the front door, the bell above the door jingled.

"Good morning," she said with her best smile, stepping aside so customers could enter. "*Komo mai.*"

Soon, the small market was full of friendly conversation. Nanea was helping a little girl open a jar of penny candy when an elderly woman asked her where she could find canned milk. "This way!" Nanea said. She felt proud to show the display she had worked so hard on.

When they reached the milk, the woman frowned. "I'd prefer the can with the red carnation. Do you have that brand?"

"Of course," Nanea said. But when she reached for the milk, she discovered a *puka,* a hole in the display. Three cans were missing, and the only ones left were not the brand the woman wanted.

"I'm sorry," Nanea said. "We're out of that kind. We had some just a few minutes ago, but . . . we have other brands. Would you like to try this one?" She pointed toward another can.

"*Tsk, tsk.* No, that won't do." The woman shook her head and walked away.

What happened to the milk? Nanea wondered. She hadn't heard the cheerful noise of the cash register, so she knew no one had purchased anything yet that morning. As she walked about the small store, smiling at customers and glancing at the items in their baskets, she was puzzled to see that no one had the missing milk. If only she could find it and please Tutu Kane's customer!

"Tutu, did you move the canned milk with the red carnation?" Nanea asked as her grandmother hurried past.

Tutu shook her head. Then she disappeared through the door to the storage room.

"Maybe the *menehune* stole it," someone said.

Nanea whirled around. A tall, thin boy leaned against the shelf behind her. He had an empty sack slung over one shoulder and his other hand tucked casually in his khaki shorts, as if he'd been standing there all day.

"The menehune?" Nanea repeated. She knew the legend of the little people who supposedly worked through the night. She could also tell from the playful twinkle in his eyes that this boy was teasing her.

Does he think I can't count cans? she thought, her cheeks burning. *That I'm not old enough to do a good job?*

When a woman asked for help with a bolt of fabric, Nanea was happy to leave the boy behind. "Yes, of course. Follow me."

As they passed the meat counter, the customer Tutu Kane was helping sounded very unhappy. "This meat is poor quality," she said. "And it's more expensive here!"

Nanea knew *that* wasn't true. Since January, the government had set limits on how much stores could charge for hard-to-get items. Tutu Kane would never sell something for higher than he should. That was against the rules.

"Perhaps you would like some fish instead," he said kindly. "It's so *'ono,* so delicious. I will show you the most fresh fish, Mrs. Hale."

Tutu Kane was so good with his customers! He always stayed positive, even when the war made things difficult. Nanea vowed to do the same. When she heard a customer complain that the mangoes weren't ripe, she hurried to the produce section.

"Do you have any ripe mangoes?" the customer asked. "Green mangoes give me a rash."

"This mango will ripen on a warm windowsill," Nanea assured her. When the woman hesitated, Nanea practiced what Tutu Kane had just taught her. "Would you like to try an orange instead?" she asked. "They're sweet and juicy. So 'ono."

But when she pointed toward the oranges, she gasped. Her perfect display was ruined. Several oranges had rolled to the floor, where one was still spinning.

As Nanea knelt to pick it up, she saw the boy in the khaki shorts quickly walking away.

Had he messed up her display? *Maybe he wants me to think the menehune were at work again,* she grumbled to herself.

But when she looked again, the boy's sack caught her eye. It wasn't empty anymore. It bulged with something round—or *several* round some-things. Oranges? Or cans of milk?

Maybe he paid for them, she thought, standing up. But one quick look at the cash register proved that he couldn't have—no one was there! Tutu was stacking bags of rice, and where was Tutu Kane? Maybe in the storage room.

Without thinking, Nanea rushed out the front door. As she stood beneath the jingling bell, she looked one way down the sidewalk and then the other.

She caught a glimpse of the boy rounding the corner on his bike, his bag of goods strapped securely over his shoulder.

And then he was gone.

As soon as Nanea stepped back inside, Tutu waved her to the back of the store. "What is it?" she asked, her eyes filled with concern.

Nanea hesitated, but she *had* to tell Tutu what she had seen. If someone was stealing from her grandparents, they needed to know! Nanea described the boy in a hushed tone, so customers wouldn't overhear.

"Did you actually see the boy steal?" asked Tutu when Nanea had finished.

Nanea lowered her eyes. "No, but—"

"Then we must not start rumors," said Tutu sternly. "We should be slow to point fingers. There has been too much of that since the war began. Isn't that right, Tutu Kane?"

As Tutu Kane stepped out of the storage room, he cupped his hand behind his ear. "Pointing fingers?" he repeated. "Yes, we should be slow to judge others. Trust more and judge less, Nanea. That is the *aloha* spirit."

Nanea's cheeks burned with shame, until Tutu Kane caught her eye and winked. "And we must be quick to put our fingers back to work. Maybe your fingers can straighten these postcards." He gestured toward the display on the checkout counter.

"Yes, Tutu Kane." She knew her grandparents were right about not starting rumors—about trusting others and not judging too quickly. But she also knew that something was *not* right about the boy in the khaki shorts.

If he came back to the store, she would keep her eye on him—until she found out just what it was.

chapter 3

Weeding Rumors

"MORE CAKE, ANYONE?" asked Tutu.

"Don't mind if I do, ma'am." The sailor across the dinner table smiled at Nanea. She had only just met Jinx, but already she liked him. He had recently arrived in Honolulu and was staying with Tutu and Tutu Kane.

"I'd like another piece, too, please!" said Nanea.

"You must have worked up quite an appetite at the store today," said Mom, tucking a piece of Nanea's hair behind her ear.

Nanea nodded as she took another bite of cake.

"We are lucky to have our granddaughter working at the market with us," said Tutu Kane. "She has more than earned her pay." He rose from the table slowly, rubbing his knees. Then he pulled a few coins from the woven *lauhala* box on a nearby shelf.

As he placed the coins into Nanea's outstretched hand, she felt proud of her hard work. Each week, she earned money for helping out at Pono's Market. And each week, she used that money to buy War Stamps. Buying War Stamps and War Bonds was like loaning money to Uncle Sam, Papa liked to say. To help the United States win the war.

But before Nanea could put the money in her pocket, Jinx asked, "May I borrow a coin?"

He took a thin dime between his fingers and inspected it. Suddenly, the dime disappeared! Jinx wiggled his fingers, as if the coin had slipped between them.

Nanea sucked in her breath. Had the coin fallen under the table?

She checked, but the floor was empty. When she sat back up, Jinx leaned forward.

"I think there's something behind your ear," he

said. "Is that a bit of coconut?"

"Oh, gosh," said Nanea, running a hand through her dark hair to wipe it clean.

But Jinx was grinning now. He reached behind her ear. When he pulled his hand back, he held the shiny dime between two fingers.

Nanea laughed out loud. "How did you do that?"

Jinx shook his head. "A magician never tells his secrets." He winked again as he took his last bite of coconut cake. "It seems I made my cake disappear, too. Thank you for a delicious dinner, Mr. and Mrs. Pono, and for inviting me to stay."

"You are very welcome," said Tutu, taking his empty plate.

"We were pleased when Lieutenant Gregory told us about you," said Tutu Kane. "You were look-ing for a room to rent, and we had one to offer."

Jinx nodded. "I was relieved to hear it, too, sir. There aren't many available rooms in Honolulu, with all the soldiers coming to the island. I wish more people were willing to open up their homes, but I'm afraid not everyone shares your—what do you call it? Your aloha spirit. Some folks are wary of soldiers."

"But why?" asked Nanea. She couldn't imagine anyone being afraid of Jinx.

"It is difficult to know who to trust during wartime," said Tutu Kane. "That's why we must *practice* trusting others. We must make it a habit. That is how we cultivate aloha."

Trust more and judge less. That's what Tutu Kane had said at the market today. Nanea studied Jinx's kind face. He was easy to trust. He was so friendly!

"How did you get your name?" she asked, hoping the question didn't sound rude.

"Jinx?" he said, settling back in his chair. "My Navy buddies call me that because I'm known to have bad luck. I'm the only sailor on my ship who doesn't know how to swim, yet somehow, I fall into the harbor more than anyone else."

Tutu Kane chuckled. "That is bad luck," he said, his eyes twinkling.

Jinx grew suddenly serious. "My luck changed the day Pearl Harbor was bombed."

Nanea held her breath and listened.

"I was onshore when the attack came," said Jinx. "And this was my good-luck charm." He pulled a smooth river rock from his pocket and handed it to Nanea. It was about the size of a silver dollar. "That was in my shirt pocket, and when a bullet hit me, it bounced off the rock and saved my life. You can feel where the bullet struck."

Nanea's fingertips found the groove made by the bullet. As she studied the rock, it grew heavy in her hands.

Tutu Kane caught her worried expression and smiled. "That's why I carry my wristwatch in my pocket. For protection. Right, Nanea?" He patted the pocket of his aloha shirt.

She giggled. "You carry that in your pocket because the strap is *broken,* Tutu Kane."

"Do I?" he asked, pretending to be puzzled. He pulled the rose-gold wristwatch from his pocket and set it on the table. "Well, it is a fine watch. I'll fix the strap one day."

Tutu clucked her tongue. "So many things broken during this war. Some we can fix, and some we must live with." Then she peered closer at the hands on Tutu Kane's watch. "It's getting late. We'll need to prepare for the blackout soon."

"That means we need to go home," Mom said to Nanea. "Let's help Tutu clean up a bit first."

Nanea jumped up. It wouldn't take long to walk the few blocks to their house, but she and her mother needed to be home by six o'clock. That was when they closed the windows, pulled the heavy, dark curtains shut, and turned off all the lights. That way, if an enemy plane flew overhead, the pilot wouldn't be able to spot lights below and use them as a target to bomb. Blacking out windows made rooms dark and stuffy, but it was the rule.

"Would you join me in the living room, Jinx?" Tutu Kane asked. "Many things are broken, but not my ukulele."

As Nanea helped Mom and Tutu clear the table, the first notes of "Hawaii Aloha" floated out from the living room. Nanea caught Tutu's eye, and they both smiled at the sweet sounds of the familiar tune.

"Weeds, weeds, weeds." Nanea's best friend, Lily Suda, yanked out a prickly weed and tossed it onto the grass. "Maybe my family and I should weed our Victory Garden more often."

The Mitchells and the Sudas had been friends for so long that they were like family. Nanea called Lily's parents Uncle Fudge and Aunt Betty, and Lily called Nanea's parents Uncle Richard and Aunt May.

Nanea hated to admit it, but the Suda's garden *had* gotten pretty weedy. Victory Gardens were a way of growing more food to help the war effort. But they were a lot of work, too.

"Maybe the Honolulu Helpers can help!" Nanea suggested.

She had started the Honolulu Helpers with a group of her friends, and so far, they had done a lot to help the war effort. They had worked in Victory Gardens all over the neighborhood and served refreshments to soldiers at USO shows, too.

"Maybe," said Lily, perking up. "It wouldn't feel like so much work if all our friends were here."

"Right!" said Nanea. She grunted as she tugged on a weed. "Oops! That's an onion." She dangled the onion in the air.

Lily grinned. "It's okay. I think we can spare one little onion. My mom said there are too many onions in Maui right now. The government shipped nine hundred tons from the mainland, and they all arrived this month. If people don't eat them, they'll rot! So everyone in Maui is sharing onion recipes."

Nanea's jaw dropped. "Nine hundred tons? Really? How many pounds is that?" She would have to do the math later, when she was working on her times tables.

Lily shrugged. "I don't know, but isn't it funny how we can have so much of one thing and not enough of another? We're skimping on butter but drowning in onions."

"At least our food isn't rationed, like it is on the mainland," said Nanea.

"Ooh, that reminds me," said Lily with a squeal. "Did I show you my birthday letter from Donna?" She fished it out of her shorts pocket. As she unfolded the pink paper, a black-and-white photo dropped out.

There was Donna, proudly showing off her latest baking creation—made without foods that were restricted because they were in short supply. "A

butterless, sugarless birthday cake for you," Donna
had written in tiny print.

"Um, yum," joked Nanea. But she studied
Donna's photo carefully. Before the war, Nanea,
Lily, and Donna had been together all the time.
The Three Kittens, Papa had called them.

Then Donna and her mother had to move back
to the mainland—to San Francisco. The government called them "nonessential citizens" and made
a new rule about who could stay and who had to
go. Mom said that with all the extra soldiers, there
were too many people on the island to feed and
house and keep safe. Losing Donna was one of the
hardest things about war. What an unfair rule!

"I wish she could be at my party next week,"
said Lily, her smile drooping.

Nanea tried to cheer her up. "Maybe we could
bake you Donna's butterless, sugarless birthday
cake," she said. "It would almost be like having her
there!"

Lily made a face, but her smile did not come back.

"Or your mom could bake something with all those onions," said Nanea, trying again. "Pineapple upside-down onion birthday cake?"

Lily finally giggled.

It felt so good to laugh together! *If only Donna were here, too,* thought Nanea.

Lily wiped her spade clean in the grass. "I'm glad gasoline is the only thing rationed in Hawaii so far," she said. "I would rather ride my bike than ride in a car anyway."

Nanea nodded. "Me, too." Now that people were given gasoline coupons and could use only a certain amount each week, they drove less and biked more. She suddenly remembered the teenage boy she had seen biking away from Pono's Market. *With stolen goods?* she wondered.

She told Lily about the boy. "I think he stole oranges and maybe milk from the market, but

I don't know for sure," she said. "And Tutu says
we shouldn't start rumors."

"Daddy says rumors are like weeds," Lily said.
"We have to pull them out before they take root."

Shame crept up Nanea's face like a sweet potato
vine, just as it had at the store when Tutu and Tutu
Kane had warned her not to point fingers. Lily's
father, Uncle Fudge, had been *hurt* by rumors—
rumors about how Japanese fishermen here on
Oahu might help the enemy. He had lost his *sampan*,
his fishing boat, because the government feared
he might use it to meet with the enemy out in the
water. Even though Uncle Fudge was an American!

Rumors can hurt people, Nanea remembered. She
hoped Lily didn't think badly of her for pointing a
finger at the teenage boy at Pono's Market.

Then Lily sat back on her heels and said, "That
boy does sound suspicious, Nanea. I think you're
right to keep an eye on him."

That made Nanea feel better. She only wanted

to protect Tutu and Tutu Kane's market. At least
Lily understood!

At the sound of a noisy jalopy pulling up out
front, Lily sprang to her feet. "Gene is home," she
said. "Since he started working with the Varsity
Victory Volunteers, he's hardly *ever* home anymore.
Let's go say hello!"

Nanea pulled off her gardening gloves and
followed Lily across the yard. She was eager to see
Lily's older brother, too. He was a good friend of
David's. But unlike David, Gene hadn't joined the
Army. He wanted to, but he couldn't—because he
was Japanese. Instead, he had joined the VVVs, a
group started by Japanese students who wanted to
serve their country during the war.

As Nanea stepped out of her muddy slippers
onto the *lanai,* or back porch, she heard Lily greet
Gene inside the house.

"*Konnichiwa!*" she called in Japanese. "What
have you been doing today, big brother?"

Nanea followed Lily into the living room just
as Gene plopped down onto the sofa. He waved
at Nanea, and his weary face broke into a smile.
"Building, building, and more building," he said.
"There's always something to build for Uncle Sam."

Nanea knew that the VVVs built roads and
warehouses at Schofield Barracks. But that was way
past Pearl Harbor, where her father worked. Gene
must have left very early in the morning to work a
full day and be home before dinner.

Aunt Betty, Lily and Gene's mom, hurried into
the room. "Ah, Gene. You're home. I'm so glad." She
kissed him and then noticed something resting on
the coffee table. "What's this?"

Gene quickly snatched it up. "It's my badge,"
he said.

"May I see your picture?" asked Lily.

Gene hesitated, but he finally handed her the
badge. Nanea caught a glimpse of his unsmiling
face in the photo, and the word "RESTRICTED"

written across the bottom of the black badge.

"Why are you restricted?" Nanea asked. As soon as the words popped out of her mouth, she wanted to take them back. She already knew the answer.

"Because I'm Japanese, of course," said Gene. "I can't join the Army. I can't even volunteer without wearing a badge that tells the world I can't be trusted. I follow all the rules, and *still* the government treats me like the enemy!"

As his voice rose, Aunt Betty shushed him. "The windows are open," she said, as if someone outside might hear.

Will he get in trouble? Nanea wondered, looking out at the street. *Would the government lock him up for speaking out?*

She remembered how Uncle Fudge had been taken away by the FBI the day of the bombing, just because he was Japanese. And some Japanese Americans were *still* being held at Sand Island, an internment camp on Oahu. *So maybe Gene is in danger, too,* she thought sadly.

Lily set Gene's badge back on the coffee table.

"Girls, have you finished your gardening?" asked Aunt Betty.

That's our signal to leave, thought Nanea. As Gene stretched out on the sofa for a nap, she cast him a sad smile.

Outside in the sunshine, Nanea felt her face flush—but not because of the heat. "I'm sorry, Lily. I didn't mean to upset your brother."

Lily shook her head. "He was already upset," she said. "Ever since he found out that he couldn't join the Army. And he hasn't been able to find a paying job, either. He wants to help out with money at home, now that Daddy can't fish anymore and works only at Mrs. Lin's crack seed shop. But Gene can't find work, not even at the shipyard. Because he's Japanese—because he looks like the enemy."

Nanea kicked at the dirt with her toes. "But

your family is just as American as mine!"

When Lily gave a sad little shrug, Nanea wished she knew how to make things better.

She had come to the Sudas' to help Lily with the garden. Now Nanea wanted to help Gene, too. She stared at the Victory Garden, where lima beans hung in clumps from leafy green plants. But right now, all she could see were the weeds.

chapter 4

Hook, Line, and Sinker

"WORK TO WIN the War!"

The poster hanging in the window of Pono's Market was beginning to peel off. Nanea carefully straightened it and added another piece of tape to the top right corner.

While she worked, she tried to ignore the furry face staring at her through the window below the poster.

A-roo!

"I see you, silly poi dog. But Tutu says you need to stay outside."

Nanea had hoped that bringing Mele to work with her would help the dog feel less lonely. At first, Mele whined more than ever. She followed every move Nanea made on the other side of the glass.

But finally, Mele had settled onto her woven mat, guarding the market like a good little watchdog.

Nanea felt like a watchdog today, too. Every time she rounded an aisle or heard a new voice, she imagined she saw the teenage boy leaning against a shelf in front of her. *Will he show up again?* she wondered.

When the bell above the front door jingled, Nanea's head jerked up from the bolt of fabric she was straightening. But it was only Mrs. Hale, the customer who had complained about the meat two days ago.

"Mr. Pono," she called in a singsong voice. "I must thank you for the fish. You were right. It was very 'ono. Do you have more?"

"Soon, Mrs. Hale. More of that delicious fish should arrive soon." Tutu Kane pulled the watch out of his pocket to check the time. "Maybe you could come back later today?"

Nanea smiled as she smoothed the floral fabric.

It was nice when Tutu Kane's kindness came back to him.

She had just finished restocking a shelf with canned meat when she heard another familiar voice. It was the voice of the teenage boy.

Nanea peeked around the shelving to see. Sure enough, the boy in the khaki shorts was talking with Tutu Kane. *About what?* she wondered. She tiptoed closer—until Tutu caught her and asked her to help sort the penny candy.

Nanea tried to do her work and watch the boy at the same time, but it was hard. She accidentally put a Tootsie Roll in the Tootsie Pop jar. Oops!

She was relieved when the boy finally waved to Tutu Kane. But he didn't leave. He wandered the aisles of the store, where Nanea couldn't watch him. When the door jingled, she looked up to see him heading outside—without buying a single thing! And yet the sack over his shoulder bulged with *something*.

Instead of getting on his bike and riding away, the boy bent down—disappearing from view. What was he doing?

The realization struck Nanea like a lightning bolt. He was petting Mele!

He wouldn't steal a dog the way he steals food, would he? she worried. She raced toward the door.

As soon as she stepped outside, the boy looked up, flashing his mischievous smile. "Is this your dog?" he asked.

"Yes," said Nanea firmly. "Mele, come." She patted her leg, but stubborn Mele stayed right where she was, enjoying an ear scratch from this boy. This *stranger.*

"It's nice to meet you, Mele," said the boy, reaching out to shake her paw. "My name is Mano."

Mano? Nanea knew that meant "shark," a slippery name for a slippery boy. *Another reason not to trust him,* she thought.

She studied the sack hanging from the

handlebars of his bike. It looked like the sack she carried her gas mask in, but there was clearly no gas mask in that bag. Whatever Mano had inside was much smaller than a mask. It rested at the very bottom, hidden from view.

So Mano didn't carry his gas mask with him, even though he was supposed to. *That's still the rule,* thought Nanea. But this boy didn't seem concerned about following rules.

When Mano straightened up, something caught her eye. Was he wearing a *bullet* on a string around his neck?

Mano caught her staring. He raised the bullet casing to his lips and blew it, like a whistle. Mele cocked her head and barked.

"I wear a bullet, and you wear a pearl," he said, gesturing toward her "Remember Pearl Harbor" pin from Papa.

Nanea quickly covered the pin with her hand. But Mano didn't seem to notice. He was too busy talking. "I found the bullet in the harbor, where I used to dive for coins. I was a diving boy— one of the best. I could swim through the strongest currents and dive in the deepest waters." He puffed out his chest.

He doesn't need to boast, thought Nanea. She had seen the diving boys for herself at Honolulu Harbor on Boat Day, when tourists tossed coins to them over the rails of boats leaving for the mainland. The boys *were* strong swimmers. She had watched them dive deep, stay underwater for what seemed like an eternity, and come up waving shiny coins to tuck into their cheeks.

But Boat Day was a thing of the past. Now the only boats that entered and left the harbor carried soldiers instead of tourists. And the pier was guarded.

"You can't dive there anymore," she pointed out.

"I *could,*" said Mano, giving her a sly smile. "But I go fishing instead."

Mele barked at the word *fish.*

"Oh, you know that word, do you?" Mano pulled something from his pocket and fed it to Mele, who gobbled it from his fingers.

"What's that?" asked Nanea. How dare he feed her dog without asking!

"Dried fish," Mano said.

And Mele barked again.

"No more," said Nanea. "That's enough now." She spoke to Mele, but her words were meant for Mano.

"It's all right. I have plenty," he said. "I know some of the best places to fish, especially at night. Sometimes I have to sneak under barbed wire"— he pointed toward a scratch on his arm—"but it's worth it."

Breaking curfew at night? Sneaking under barbed wire? Nanea couldn't believe it. Mano was breaking all *sorts* of rules. And he was bragging about it!

Tutu's face suddenly appeared in the window,

searching for Nanea. When she saw Mano, she waved kindly at him. Mano grinned and waved back.

Nanea wanted to catch Tutu's eye, to warn her that this boy wasn't a friend. That he was taking advantage of her and Tutu Kane's kindness! But they seemed to have fallen for this slippery boy, hook, line, and sinker.

Mele had, too. She jumped up on his legs, sniffing at his pocket.

"Down, Mele. Bad girl!" Nanea scolded.

Mano didn't seem to mind. "I'll come back and visit again," he said as he began to wheel his bike away.

Nanea dropped to her knees and wrapped her arms around Mele's neck. "You stay with me, girl," she whispered.

As Mano waved and climbed onto his bike, Mele strained to follow him.

"No, Mele!" said Nanea. Usually her dog was a

good judge of character. "You're letting your nose—and your belly—deceive you this time."

She pretended to pull a burr out of Mele's fur, but secretly, she watched Mano pedal off down the street. She was surprised when he braked to a stop in front of Andrada's Market a couple of blocks away. He carefully parked his bike, grabbed his canvas sack, and headed inside.

Uh-oh. Was Mano going to steal from friendly Mr. Andrada, too?

As she waited for Mano to come back out, she held her breath like a diving boy. Mele's body felt tense, too, wrapped within Nanea's arms. They waited together.

Then the door to Andrada's Market flung back open. Nanea let go—for only a second—and Mele took off like a shot down the street.

Nanea sprinted after her, but by the time she reached Mele, the hungry dog already had her nose in Mano's pocket. "Mele, no!" Nanea cried.

Mano smiled and raised his finger to his lips, silencing Nanea. But why?

He nodded his head toward the door of Andrada's Market. A loud, angry voice spilled out from within.

"You mark my words, the government is going to start rationing meat like they do gasoline," a woman was saying. "When they do, they're just going to fuel the black market. And I won't blame customers who decide to do their shopping there!"

As a man responded in hushed tones, Mano raised an eyebrow and grinned at Nanea. He seemed to be enjoying the fight.

"We shouldn't eavesdrop," whispered Nanea. But as she quickly led Mano away from the shop entrance, she had to ask the question niggling at her. "What's the black market?"

His eyes lit up, as if he couldn't wait to tell her. "It's a way to buy things that are hard to get, like gasoline," he explained. "You can get as much gasoline as you want, you know—even without ration coupons. As long as you're willing to pay more money for it."

Nanea wrinkled her forehead. "But isn't that against the law?" she asked. "Isn't gasoline rationed so we all have what we need?"

Mano shrugged. "Sure," he said.

He knows an awful lot about this "black market," thought Nanea. *Who is this boy with the bullet around his neck who breaks rules so easily?*

As she carried Mele back to Pono's Market, she was relieved to see Mano ride the other way.

She hoped that shark wouldn't be circling around Pono's Market anymore.

chapter 5

The Shark Goddess

A-ROO! A-ROO! MELE barked.

"Shhh," Nanea whispered. "Not so loud! We should knock first." She made her dog sit on the lanai before she rapped gently on Tutu's back door.

It was Saturday morning, and hula lessons wouldn't start for another hour. Mary Lou was still home sleeping, but Nanea had come early. How could she sleep in when her thoughts kept floating back to that slippery Mano?

"Nanea?" Tutu's worried face appeared in the doorway. "So early today! Is everything all right?"

Nanea nodded. As she hugged Tutu, she breathed in the reassuring scent of her grand-mother's talcum powder and coffee. Nanea smiled. Already, she felt better.

"May I practice early?" she asked. "Before the others arrive?"

Tutu seemed surprised, but pleased. "Of course," she said. "But come inside a moment. I'm just putting away the breakfast dishes."

As Nanea followed Tutu into the kitchen, Tutu Kane pushed away from the table. "Who is this? Nanea? I thought it was a zebra dove chirping in the backyard."

Nanea giggled. "Good morning, Tutu Kane. Are you going to the market?"

"Yes. It's time," he said. Then he patted his shirt pocket. "I *think* it's time. I've misplaced my watch."

Tutu tsk-tsked. "We'll find it. But not right now. Our customers will be waiting for you."

"Is Jinx here?" Nanea asked, hoping to say hello to the sailor.

"No. He leaves very early," said Tutu. "So it will just be you and me. *Makaukau?* Are you ready?" Tutu asked.

"*Ae*," said Nanea, turning back toward the porch. "Yes. I'm ready."

Soon the lyrics to "Waikiki" drifted up from Tutu's phonograph. The melody was Hawaiian, but the words were sung in English, which would be easy for soldiers to understand at the USO show next Saturday.

Nanea listened to the music and stepped her feet from right to left, doing the *kaholo*. Her body followed the song about beautiful Waikiki Beach. She swept her arm in front of her as lightly as a breeze drifting across the sand. She raised both arms into the air and brought them softly down, like shadows falling in the night. But as she cupped her hand behind her ear, listening for the rolling surf, she heard something else.

In her mind she heard Mano again, boasting of how he broke the rules. Telling her how he snuck under the barbed-wire fence at night to go fishing in the sea.

Nanea had come here to forget Mano. Usually, hula took her mind off her troubles. But today, that slippery shark had swum right into her hula!

When the music stopped abruptly, she glanced toward the phonograph, where Tutu had lifted the needle from the record.

"What is it, Tutu?"

"Your mind isn't on the story," Tutu gently scolded. "When your mind wanders, your hands and feet do, too. Where is your mind this morning, keiki?"

Nanea's face fell. How could she tell Tutu that her mind was on the mysterious boy who dove for bullets and dodged barbed-wire fences? She had tried once, and Tutu had told her not to point fingers.

But she didn't want to lie. "I'm sorry, Tutu. I was thinking about . . . a shark."

Tutu tilted her head. "A shark?"

"Yes." Then Nanea had an idea. "Will you tell

me one of your stories, Tutu? About sharks?"

Tutu often told Hawaiian legends about gods and goddesses of the island. Maybe Tutu could tell a story that would help Nanea know what to do about Mano!

Tutu's eyes crinkled into a smile. "Come sit," she said, patting the seat beside her. "I will tell you about the shark goddess *Ka'ahupahau*." As Tutu began her story, her warm, steady voice filled the lanai. Even outside the window, Mele's ears perked up from where she lay resting in the early-morning sun.

"The shark goddess Ka'ahupahau guarded the entrance of Pearl Harbor with her brother, *Kahi'uka*," explained Tutu.

Nanea nodded. She had heard Tutu tell the story of Ka'ahupahau and Kahi'uka before, and she was eager to hear it again.

"She was born a human with fire-red hair. But as a shark, her body could take many forms. She could become a net, difficult to tear. And with her net body, she captured man-eating sharks that entered her harbor."

Like Mano? wondered Nanea. She wished she could catch him, too—prove that he was a thief!

"Her brother Kahi'uka struck the man-eating sharks with his tail," Tutu continued. "His tail was *very* sharp."

As she flicked her hand sideways, demonstrating the shark tail, Nanea leaned backward. And she thought of her own brother, David, and her constant wish. *If only he were here now.*

"Ka'ahupahau and Kahi'uka were not man-eating sharks, so the people of Oahu fed them and scraped the barnacles off their backs." Tutu slid her hand down the back of her arm, demonstrating. "And in return, Ka'ahupahau and her brother protected the harbor and the people."

Just like I want to protect Tutu and Tutu Kane, thought Nanea. As silence fell, she wondered aloud.

"Is Ka'ahupahau still there, Tutu?"

Her grandmother smiled. "Some say she is still there today, guarding the harbor. Protecting her people."

Nanea's mind swirled like the rolling surf. *I'm like the shark goddess Ka'ahupahau,* she realized. *I'm going to protect my 'ohana, my family.*

The shark goddess Ka'ahupahau had her brother to help her. But even without David, Nanea was determined to find a way.

"Mary Lou, are you listening?"

"Hmm?"

As the girls packed up their things after hula lessons, Nanea was trying to tell Mary Lou about the legend of the shark goddess. *David isn't here, but Mary Lou is. Can she help me keep Pono's Market safe from Mano the shark?* Nanea wondered.

"I said that Ka'ahupahau guards Pearl Harbor

from man-eating sharks. Did you know that?"

Mary Lou didn't answer. She was studying a framed photograph hanging on the wall of Tutu's porch. "This *holoku* looks like a wedding gown, don't you think?"

"What?" Why was Mary Lou talking about weddings when Nanea was trying to tell her something important?

She glanced over her sister's shoulder. The hula dancer in the photo was wearing a holoku, a floor-length hula gown with a long train of fabric that floated out behind her. It *did* look like a wedding dress, but that was beside the point.

"Ka'ahupahau's brother guards the harbor, too, with his sharp, spiky tail. Like this!" Nanea tried to flick her wrist the way Tutu had.

But Mary Lou didn't notice. She spun in a slow circle, as if she were wearing a holoku. "There haven't been any weddings for a while now."

Nanea sighed. Clearly, Mary Lou wasn't going

to help her guard the harbor. It sounded like Mary Lou was ready to swim off and *marry* any man-eating sharks that came her way!

"Since when do you care so much about weddings?" Nanea asked.

Mary Lou shrugged. "I just miss the wedding *luaus*. Remember how many there were when soldiers started going off to war seven months ago?"

Nanea nodded. "But we had a luau for David's birthday just last month." She could almost smell the *kalua* pig roasting in the *imu,* and the memory made her mouth water.

As Tutu stepped onto the porch, she clucked her tongue. "Now the government urges us not to have birthday luaus. Only luaus for weddings and to welcome our soldiers home from war."

"Really?" said Nanea. Here was another change. Another rule. There were so many!

But Mary Lou didn't seem to care. "See? We need more weddings then." She smiled and took another spin in her imaginary gown.

Weddings, weddings, weddings. Nanea fought down an exasperated sigh. "Are you almost ready to go, Mary Lou? We need to take Mele home before I go to Pono's Market."

From just outside the porch door, Mele whined. Sometimes Nanea was sure that dog could understand everything she said.

"Isn't Mele coming to the market with you today?" asked Tutu.

Nanea shook her head. "She's too much work." What she *didn't* say is that Mele would be safer at home—away from boys who fill their pockets with dried fish.

No. If Mano comes back to the market today, he won't be visiting with Mele, thought Nanea, setting her jaw.

Like the shark goddess, Nanea would keep that shark out of the harbor, away from the people—and dog—she loved.

chapter 6
The Black Market

AS SOON AS Mom pulled up in front of Pono's
Market that afternoon, Nanea jumped out of the
car. She waited until Tutu had stepped out of the
car, too. Then she pushed through the front door,
setting off the jingling bell. "I'm sorry we're late!"
she called to Tutu Kane, who stood near the cash
register.

When Nanea saw the customer on the other side
of the counter, she stopped short. It was Mano.

"Komo mai," he teased, as if he were the one
working at the market and welcoming customers.

Anger rose through Nanea like heat from the
stones in an imu pit. How could Mano's words get
to her so easily?

She wouldn't let him see. She pasted on a smile

and went straight for her apron, hanging on the hook. Then she reached for the feather duster and began dusting a shelf near the checkout counter. That way, she could keep an eye on Mano.

"I've already dusted, Nanea," said Tutu Kane. "Would you sweep out front, please?"

Nanea wanted to protest. But what could she say? She grabbed the broom, gave Mano one last look over her shoulder, and stepped outside.

She was surprised when he followed her out.

"Where's Mele?" he asked, disappointment flashing across his face.

"At home," Nanea said simply. "Where she won't run away."

Mano patted his pocket. "That's too bad. I brought her extra fish today."

Nanea said nothing. She swept faster and harder, pushing a pile of dirt into the street. And she waited for Mano to go away.

But he didn't.

"You're working so hard," he said. "Are you try-ing to win the war?"

"What?" Nanea stopped sweeping.

Mano pointed toward the poster in the window. Then she saw the mischief in his eyes. He was teas-ing her—about working hard!

"I *do* work hard," she said. "I help here at the market. I visit wounded soldiers and perform at hula shows to make them feel better. I weed Victory Gardens. My friends and I are even going to plant one for my tutus tomorrow!" Once she started talk-ing, the words flowed like lava. Then a few more bubbled up to the surface. "What are *you* doing to help win the war?"

Mano leaned back, as if he could feel the heat of her words.

He didn't answer right away.

Maybe now he'll leave, thought Nanea. She began to sweep again, with short, strong strokes.

"I help the soldiers, too," Mano finally said.

"I get them whatever they ask for, anytime they ask for it. Food. Cigarettes. Even at night. I know how to sneak past patrol officers on the beach, and how to get past their patrol dogs, too." He patted the fish in his pocket with a sly smile. "I used to get my coins by diving in the harbor, but *now* I get them by doing favors for soldiers. I've earned as much as a half dollar in just one run."

Nanea's ears burned. This boy was boasting again about breaking the rules.

And where is he getting those cigarettes and that food? she wondered. *What market is he stealing from?*

She couldn't listen to another boastful word. "I have work to do," she said, brushing past him and back into Pono's Market.

When she felt him follow her in, her heart raced.

"Do you need help planting the Victory Garden?" he asked.

She whirled around to face him. "What?"

"I can help with gardening," he said.

Nanea could barely answer. "N-no," she sput-
tered. "No, we don't need help." *Not from a thief. Not
from a rule breaker.*

Then she felt a hand on her shoulder.

Tutu Kane spoke. "Are you looking for work,
Mano?"

"Yes, Mr. Pono," said Mano, ducking his head
politely.

"Come to my house tomorrow afternoon then.
Mrs. Pono and I may have a job for you."

A job? What job—gardening? Nanea wondered
with horror if Tutu Kane had just invited Mano to
help her with the Victory Garden.

Mano smiled broadly. "Mahalo, Mr. Pono.
Thank you." After writing down Tutu Kane's
address, he waved at Nanea and disappeared from
the shop.

Nanea couldn't look at Tutu Kane. Didn't he
know what kind of boy Mano was? Now he had
invited Mano to his *home*!

When Tutu Kane stepped in front of Nanea and held both of her shoulders, she had to face him.

His words were stern. "Sometimes, Nanea, it is as important to accept help as it is to offer it. Mano needs work, as many do during this war. And we have work to give—work to share with him. We help him by letting him help us. Do you understand?"

She *didn't* understand. Couldn't Tutu Kane see the trouble this slippery boy might bring?

She had tried to tell her grandparents once, when she first suspected Mano of stealing. But they had told her not to judge too quickly—not to start rumors. Tutu Kane trusted Mano, because that was the spirit of aloha.

But Nanea *couldn't* trust this boy. He had broken too many rules! How could she show Tutu Kane the truth about Mano?

I need to catch him in a strong, sturdy net, she reminded herself, thinking of the shark goddess.

I need to catch him stealing or breaking the rules. Then Tutu Kane will listen!

Thump!

When Nanea heard the Sunday newspaper hit the porch steps, she slipped out of bed and through the living room. The house seemed so quiet. Was Papa home yet from work? She couldn't tell.

She opened the front door quietly and stepped past the pile of shoes on the porch. The steps felt cold beneath her bare feet. As she hit the last step, she nearly landed on an anthill teeming with tiny ants.

"Where did you come from?" she asked, peering closer. One ant seemed to be carrying a crumb three times its size. "I know how you feel," she said. Her worries felt heavy this morning, too.

Today was the day when Mano would go to Tutu and Tutu Kane's house. *At least I'll be there to keep an eye on him,* she thought. *Me, Lily, and the rest of the Honolulu Helpers.* So far, Lily was the only one she had told about Mano. Nanea couldn't wait to see her friend and catch her up on everything that had happened.

She reached for the *Honolulu Advertiser* newspaper, careful not to disturb the anthill, and then headed back up the porch steps.

"Good morning, Nanea."

It was Mrs. Lin from next door. *Tap, tap, tap.* As she began to walk over with her cane, Nanea could tell her elderly neighbor was eager for conversation.

Nanea took a deep breath and greeted her kindly. "Good morning, Mrs. Lin. How are you today?"

"Fine, fine. I saw the advertisement in the paper this morning about a shipment of apples coming next week. Will your tutus be selling them?"

Mrs. Lin seemed to think that Nanea had secret information because she worked at Pono's Market.

And Mrs. Lin liked to be the first to know about things like this. Then she could tell all the other aunties on the block.

"I'm sorry, Mrs. Lin. I don't know—"

"Turn the page," said Mrs. Lin, gesturing toward the newspaper. "I'll show you."

Nanea flipped through the paper until Mrs. Lin spotted the ad. "There, next to the ads for the soldiers." She clucked her tongue, looking at the full page of ads. "Ads for inexpensive meals, and rooms at our hotels, and markets filled with cheap souvenirs. Some of these soldiers take, take, take. And when they leave Oahu, there will be nothing left."

Nanea didn't know what to say. Was Mrs. Lin angry with the soldiers? Maybe she was one of the people Jinx had talked about—people here in Honolulu who weren't happy to see so many soldiers.

But soldiers are Americans! thought Nanea sadly. *They're serving their country, just like David.*

Nanea knew that Japanese Americans like Gene were being treated unfairly. But she hadn't known that some soldiers were, too. She hoped David wasn't one of them.

Nanea swallowed her thoughts and said as brightly as she could, "I'll ask Tutu Kane when he will be selling the apples, okay?"

"Yes, yes," said Mrs. Lin. "Thank you, Nanea." And then she was on her way, tapping back across the dirt yard toward her home.

Nanea folded the newspaper back together and hurried inside, where she found Papa sitting at the kitchen table. She felt lighter just seeing him, like an ant that had finally dropped its heavy crumb.

She tiptoed in behind Papa and gave him her special hug, wrapping her arms tightly around him and squeezing twice. That was their code for "Buddies forever." When Papa's whiskers scratched her face, she didn't even mind.

"Good morning, Sunshine," he said with a

yawn. "It's so good to be home again."

She kissed his cheek and then laid the *Honolulu Advertiser* on the breakfast table before him, wishing the paper still looked neat and tidy. "Too many double shifts!" she said, sliding into a seat beside him.

"Indeed," said Papa. "I think you've grown two inches since I saw you last." He waggled his eyebrows at her.

Nanea giggled. "No, I haven't, silly Papa." But she *did* feel as if she'd grown a little. So much had happened in such a short time.

While Papa sipped his coffee and read the front page of the newspaper, she read one of the middle sections. Then she spotted an ad showing a pantry overflowing with canned goods. "Hoarding is unpatriotic," the ad read.

The pile of cans reminded her of Mano's lumpy backpack.

She glanced sideways at Papa. Could she tell

him about Mano? Tutu and Tutu Kane had scolded her so sharply when she pointed the finger. Papa might, too.

So instead, she asked, "Papa, what's hoarding? Is it like selling things on the black market?"

His eyes widened. "What do *you* know about the black market, Nanea?"

She quickly shrugged. "Not very much."

Papa looked relieved. He cleared his throat. "Well, let's see. Hoarding is when people stock up on more food than they actually need," he explained. "We might not need to ration food here on Oahu if we all share—if we buy only as much food as our family needs each week. That way there's enough left over for other people to buy, too."

Nanea nodded. She had seen people buy more than they needed at Pono's Market and not leave enough of certain things for other customers.

Papa rubbed his chin. "And the black market is

where people buy and sell some of the things that we *don't* have enough of, like gasoline, for very high prices."

"Where do they get the things to sell? Do they steal them?" Nanea asked, thinking again of Mano.

Papa nodded. "Sometimes."

"But that's against the rules!" She sat forward in her chair. "I don't understand how some people can break the rules so easily. It's not right."

Papa put his hand on hers. "People do things for lots of reasons—reasons we don't always know about. So instead of judging other people, we should just try to make the best decisions that *we* can. Right, Sunshine?"

Nanea wasn't so sure she agreed. *What could be a good reason to steal?* But before she could ask Papa, her sister padded into the kitchen.

"Where's Mom?" Mary Lou let out a giant yawn as she cracked open the refrigerator door.

"She's doing a sewing project with the Red

Cross," said Papa. "And good morning to you, too."

Mary Lou glanced up. "Papa!" she said. "I'm sorry." She came over to give him a big hug.

"Late night?" he asked.

She nodded. "We served banana splits at the USO. Did you know the USO in Honolulu is famous for its banana splits? They sometimes go through two hundred gallons of ice cream in a single day!"

Papa smiled. "I might have heard about that."

Nanea scrunched up her forehead. "Two hundred gallons? Isn't that hoarding?"

Mary Lou looked horrified. "No! Not if it's for the soldiers."

The rules were all so confusing. Nanea was starting to feel like a banana herself, split in two.

Papa stood up and smothered a yawn. "Time for my beauty sleep," he joked. After working the night shift, he sometimes slept all day. "Will I see my beautiful girls later today?"

Nanea nodded. "But first I'm planting a Victory

Garden at Tutu and Tutu Kane's."

"Well I'm proud of you," said Papa. "You're carrying on the Mitchell family farming tradition. In fact, I have something special you can use." He waved his hand for her to follow.

Papa led Nanea out to the garage, where gardening tools were neatly stored on shelves. He picked up a spade. "This was Grandmom Mitchell's," he said. "She sent it to me shortly after your mom and I were married—a piece of my home in Oregon as we started our own home here in Hawaii. It's old, but it's sturdy."

Nanea stroked the navy blue handle, worn smooth beneath her grandmother's and father's fingers. She couldn't wait to use it today!

"Mahalo, Papa," she said. "Thank you." Holding that special spade, she almost forgot all about Mano.

Almost.

chapter 7

A Shark in the Harbor

TUTU'S BACKYARD SMELLED of ginger and carnations, like always. But it looked very different now that Tutu Kane had dug a dark rectangle of fresh earth in the middle of the yard.

Nanea was relieved to see that Mano wasn't here yet.

"Maybe he won't come at all," she whispered to Lily. She had told Lily all about Mano's visits to the market on the walk over to Tutu and Tutu Kane's. It felt so good to talk to someone who believed her!

"Maybe not," said Lily, her eyes wide.

"When you water the garden, be careful not to get water in the air-raid shelter," said Tutu. She pointed toward the deep hole in the ground a few feet away. "We don't want it to fill up or cave in."

"Yes, Tutu," said Nanea. "We'll be careful." She already dreaded climbing into backyard shelters during air-raid drills. If one of those shelters were damp and dripping with water and worms, it would be even worse!

While they waited for the other Honolulu Helpers to arrive, Nanea and Lily unpacked the tools they had brought: Five pairs of gloves. Three shiny hand trowels. And two spades—including the special one that Papa had loaned Nanea just this morning.

Tutu Kane came out of the garage carrying larger tools, too: a shovel and a long rake.

"Mahalo, Tutu Kane. Now we have everything we need!" said Nanea—just as the other Honolulu Helpers burst through the back gate.

"I have seeds!" said Dixie, waving a brown paper bag. "Beans and carrots."

"I have turnips!" shouted Alani, waving a bag of her own. Bernice was close on her heels.

Nanea was glad so many of her friends had shown up to *kokua*—to help. "Let's get started!" she said happily.

Pretty soon, she was using Grandmom Mitchell's spade to dig small holes. "Nine holes times seven rows equals . . . sixty-three plants," she announced, practicing her multiplication skills.

"I sure hope I have sixty-three seeds!" said Bernice, who followed behind dropping in the tiny seeds.

When Dixie started dancing the jitterbug with Tutu Kane's rake, everyone laughed. But as she twirled in a circle, she accidentally knocked two lime-green mangoes off the tree overhead.

"Oh, no!" Alani quickly picked them up and wiped them off with the hem of her shirt. "They're not ripe enough to eat."

"They're pretty green," agreed Nanea. "A customer at Pono's Market said she gets a rash from eating green mangoes."

Bernice wiped sweat from her brow with the back of her garden glove. "I had that once. I got blisters around my mouth and on my hands. They hurt so much!"

Nanea grimaced. "Then we should definitely put these in a sunny spot so they can finish ripening."

As she placed the mangoes on Tutu's porch steps, she hoped they would turn reddish-yellow—that they wouldn't go to waste.

When she turned back toward the garden, she heard the sound she'd been dreading: the creak of a bike chain. As the dark-haired boy pulled up along-side Tutu's fence, a tingle ran down Nanea's spine.

Mano.

The shark that had been circling Pono's Market was now lurking just outside Tutu's backyard.

He stood on the other side of the gate, but Nanea didn't let him in. Like the shark goddess, she would protect her harbor. *You won't hurt my 'ohana,* she wanted to say. *Not on my watch.* She wished she had a sharp tail like Kahi'uka and could swat that boy far, far away.

"Komo mai, Mano," Tutu called from the steps of the lanai. "Nanea, invite him in, please. He's here to paint the fence."

When Tutu Kane came out of the garage carrying a pail of paint, Nanea sighed deeply and reached for the gate. The white paint on the fence *had* worn thin in some spots, she noticed. But she'd rather repaint it herself than have this slippery boy in her grandparents' yard.

As Nanea returned to the garden, she saw Lily cast Mano a wary glance. *At least Lily knows he can't be trusted,* Nanea told herself. Both girls watched Mano with careful eyes.

Dixie was the first to speak to him. "Is Mano your real name?" she asked.

Mano looked up from his paintbrush and flashed her a smile. "It is now. My friends call me Mano because I'm a good fisherman, like my father."

Lily was suddenly all ears, Nanea could tell. *Is it because her father is a fisherman, too?* Nanea wondered.

"Are you Japanese?" Lily asked Mano.

Such direct questions! Nanea couldn't believe how bold her friends were being. But she had to admit, she was just as curious as they were to hear what Mano would say.

He didn't answer right away. He took a long, slow stroke with his paintbrush. Then he said, "My father is Japanese. My mother was Hawaiian. And my great-grandfather—after he died, he came back to us. As a *shark*."

He glanced sideways at the girls, as if he knew he had just hooked them and could reel them into shore.

Nanea patted dirt over a freshly planted seed. She wouldn't let Mano see that she was interested.

This boastful storyteller had enough of an audience without her.

But as he spoke of his great-grandfather, the shark, she found herself drawn in. Mano painted a picture in her mind with his words as easily as he painted Tutu Kane's fence.

"He protected my 'ohana from danger and provided them with great gifts. When my tutu kane cast his fishing net, the shark chased all the smaller fish into the net. When Tutu Kane pulled in the net, it was *full* of fish." Mano spread out his hands to show the bulging fishing net.

Like your canvas sack, Nanea thought. Through the slats of the fence, she could see the sack hanging empty from the handlebars of Mano's bicycle. What was he planning to fill it with today? Would he steal from Tutu and Tutu Kane?

"Where do you live?" Dixie blurted. "I haven't seen you at school before."

Mano painted a few more strokes on the fence

and then said, "I live near the beach in Waikiki." He cast a mysterious glance over his shoulder and added, "In a palace by the sea."

A palace? Nanea scoffed. But she couldn't help imagining what his "palace" might look like. Would it be dark and hidden from view? Full of treasure chests and stolen loot?

Stop it! she scolded herself. *Don't get reeled in.* This boy told interesting stories. But that didn't change who he was.

"I know another shark story," she said quickly, before Mano could go on. "Do you know of the shark goddess Ka'ahupahau?" she asked her friends.

She was grateful when Lily shook her head no.

Nanea tried to tell the story as Tutu had. She spoke slowly and acted out the movements with her hands, as if she were doing a hula.

When she finished, Nanea saw that Mano was grinning at her. "I know something else about

Ka'ahupahau, the shark goddess," he said, his voice taunting.

Nanea wasn't about to take the bait.

But Dixie did. "What?" she asked eagerly.

Mano kept his eyes on Nanea. "Ka'ahupahau tried to keep the man-eaters out of the harbor," he said. "But she could not *always* tell the good sharks from the bad." He held Nanea's gaze for another moment before turning back to his painting.

Nanea's cheeks burned. *Why did he look at me when he said that?* she wondered. *Does he think I can't tell the good sharks from the bad?*

While her friends chattered around her like mynah birds, Nanea unwound the hose and watered the garden in silence.

When Tutu called the girls inside for warm guava bread, Nanea jumped up. She was eager to talk to Lily inside, away from Mano. But as soon as she reached the door, Tutu waved her back out.

"Please invite Mano in for bread, too," said Tutu.

As Nanea turned and crossed the yard toward him, her feet felt heavy.

"Tutu says there's guava bread for you, too," she said to Mano. She expected him to come right away—to stop working and to devour his share of bread, or *more* than his share.

But he didn't. He smiled at her and waved his paintbrush. "Please tell Mrs. Pono mahalo, but that I would like to finish my work."

Nanea nodded, relieved. But as she turned to go, he asked, "Where is your pin today, *Momi*?"

Momi was the Hawaiian word for "pearl," like the pearl on Nanea's pin from Papa. The affectionate nickname caught her by surprise. How dare Mano treat her as if he knew her so well?

"I left my pin at home so that I wouldn't lose it in the garden," she said simply. *Or so that it wouldn't be stolen!* she wanted to add.

Nanea turned and ran back toward Tutu's house without saying good-bye. *Maybe Ka'ahupahau couldn't always tell the good sharks from the bad,* she thought, *but I can.* And right now, she wanted to get as far away from that bad shark as she could.

As Nanea carried the empty plates to the kitchen sink, she heard a knock on the back door. Her stomach twisted. Was it Mano? Had he changed his mind about coming inside?

But when Tutu Kane answered the door, Nanea was relieved to see a smiling sailor standing outside. "Jinx!"

"I just saw the most amazing thing," he said, his eyes twinkling. "A Victory Garden that appeared from out of nowhere. *Poof!* Just like magic."

Nanea giggled. "My friends and I planted it today." She wished they were all still there so that she could introduce them to Jinx, but most of the Honolulu Helpers had gone home. Only Lily stood beside her now, staring shyly at the sailor from beneath her shiny black bangs.

Nanea leaned toward Lily and said, "Jinx knows how to do magic tricks."

"Only one or two," said the sailor. "It's a pleasure to meet you, miss." He reached out his hand to Lily, but when she went to shake it, he opened his fingers and a pink carnation sprang up.

"Oh!" Lily squealed in surprise, then laughed and took the flower.

Tutu Kane chuckled. "Perhaps you could make my watch reappear," he said to Jinx. "I'm a boat adrift at sea without it."

Jinx tapped one closed fist on top of the other, as if he were trying. Nanea watched carefully. But when he opened his fingers, his palms were empty. "I'm sorry," he said, bowing his head. "My magic is only so powerful."

Tutu Kane sighed. "Mahalo. Thank you for trying." He winked at Nanea.

As Jinx accepted a thick slice of guava bread

from Tutu, he asked, "Did you girls also paint the fence? It's looking particularly white today."

Nanea's smile faded.

"We hired a young boy to do the painting," explained Tutu. "A very hard worker."

"Well, he did a good job," said Jinx. "It looks like a layer of frosting on our favorite coconut cake." He grinned at Nanea.

Tutu Kane nodded thoughtfully. "Yes, he did a fine job. Maybe we can talk to the neighbors. Find more jobs for him to do."

As Lily's eyes met hers, Nanea's throat tightened. *More jobs?* She couldn't bear the thought of Mano coming anywhere near her grandparents' home again! She quickly changed the subject. "Are you having a birthday cake at your party tomorrow, Lily?"

Her friend nodded. "And Mom is making *mochi*."

Nanea's mouth watered just thinking about

Aunt Betty's sticky rice cakes. "Lily's mom makes the best mochi," she told Jinx.

"Is that so?" he said. "Well, I hope I'll have the chance to try it one day."

"You could come to my party!" Lily blurted. She sat back, as if she had surprised even herself with the invitation. "I mean, I'll ask Mom and Daddy if you can. But I think they'll say yes."

Nanea grinned. *Lily likes Jinx as much as I do!*

"You could come with us," said Tutu kindly.

Jinx smiled. "Well, don't mind if I do. I never turn down a party—or cake." He patted his stomach.

When it was time to walk home, Nanea and Lily were still talking about the party. "Maybe Jinx will do more magic tricks!" said Nanea as she hurried down the back porch steps.

Her feet were moving so quickly that she nearly tripped over a mango. "Oops! Maybe we should put this somewhere else." She picked up the green fruit.

"Where did the other one go?" asked Lily. "Did you throw it out?"

Nanea checked the step again. Lily was right—the second mango was missing. She checked under the step to see if it had wobbled off. "That's strange. Maybe an army of ants ran away with it."

But as the girls began to pack up their garden tools, Nanea realized that the mango wasn't the only thing missing. "Lily, have you seen my spade? The one with the blue wooden handle?"

Lily tucked her hair behind her ear and searched the ground near the garden.

"No. Did someone else take it home?"

Nanea shrugged. "No one else brought tools. That was our job, remember?"

The girls searched Tutu Kane's garage. And beneath the flower bushes. And along the fence line. As they searched, Nanea felt her spirits sink. "Grandmom Mitchell's special spade is lost! Just like Tutu Kane's watch."

Then an idea struck. "Or maybe it's not lost. Maybe someone *stole* it," she whispered to Lily. She gestured toward the freshly painted fence.

Lily's eyes widened.

Nanea knew better than to say it out loud. *Rumors are like weeds. We have to pull them out before they take root,* she reminded herself.

But her worries about Mano had already taken root. Too much had happened; too many things had gone missing. Food from the market. Her spade and the mango. Even Tutu Kane's watch. Had Mano stolen that, too, while talking with Tutu Kane at the market?

And now Tutu and Tutu Kane wanted him to do *more* work for them! If Nanea didn't do something soon, what would happen next?

chapter 8

An Unexpected Guest

MONDAY WAS A day of *waiting*. Waiting for the postman to bring a letter from David. Waiting for Papa to wake up from his nap so that they could go to the Sudas' for Lily's party. Waiting to tell Lily that the spade was still missing. Nanea had called all of the Honolulu Helpers, but none of them had her special spade.

Because a slippery shark swam away with it! thought Nanea. She had to find a way to catch him in the act—to cast her net and trap him, once and for all. But how?

A noise just outside the front door made her jump. But the tone of Mele's bark told her that it was someone familiar.

"Is that the postman?" she asked, jumping up.

Sure enough, when she opened the front door, she saw Mr. Cruz disappearing around the corner. And a letter waited for her inside the mailbox.

Nanea recognized the handwriting immediately. It was from David!

For a split second, she thought about saving the letter for later, when Mary Lou would be home from the USO and they could open it together. *But I've been waiting all day,* she reminded herself. She was tired of waiting!

Nanea tore open the envelope, ripping through the "Censored" stamp in the corner. When she pulled out the letter, she was disappointed to see a hole in it—a puka, where some of David's precious words had been.

"Mom, look how much of David's letter got cut out!" she complained, carrying the letter into the kitchen.

"Oh, dear," said Mom with a tense smile. "It looks as if David wrote something the Army didn't want others to read—about military plans or what he's doing in basic training."

Nanea blew out a breath of frustration. "I've been waiting for days for a letter from him! And now half the words are missing."

"I know, honey," said Mom. She patted the chair beside her. "Just remember: It's easy to forget the rules about what we can say and what we can't."

Nanea slid into the seat. She knew Mom was right. Forgetting the rules was different from breaking them on purpose—like *some* boys did.

She sighed and started at the beginning of the letter, reading aloud so that Mom could hear, too.

Dear Nanea,

How is your summer going, baby sis? It sounds like you are working hard. Make sure you spend a few sunny days at the beach with Lily, too. And if you see my buddy Darrell there, tell him I say hello.

I've met some good guys here at boot camp, and I'm

looking forward to the day when we can fight the enemy.

Nanea swallowed hard, her eyes blurring over the word *enemy*.

"The next part got cut out," she said, holding up the paper and peering at Mom through the hole.

"That's all right," said Mom. "What else does he say?"

"Something about you," said Nanea, reading ahead.

Tell Mom that they're feeding me well here, but I'm getting tired of pork and beans. I miss her pineapple upside-down cake, Tutu's two-finger poi, and Pop's kalua pig. I swear I can smell that pig roasting all the way over here in Mississippi!

I have to get my beauty sleep now. Be good, Monkey. Keep my room clean, and give Mele a hug for me.

Yours,

David

Nanea pressed the letter to her face, hoping to smell David's Old Spice aftershave. She smelled nothing, but she kept the letter in front of her eyes to hide hot tears.

Monkey.

David was the only one who called her Monkey, and she hadn't heard her nickname for more than three weeks! She could picture him saying it and flashing her his movie-star smile.

Mom kissed the top of Nanea's head. "I miss him too, honey," she said. "Do you want to bring the letter to Lily's?"

Nanea wiped her eyes and nodded. "I'll put it with her present so I remember." She hurried to her bedroom, where the small, pale blue gift rested on her dresser.

Nanea took a moment to straighten the ribbon. Lily had told her that with Japanese gift-giving, the outside of the present is just as important as the inside. So Nanea had wrapped the gift carefully.

As she left her room, she nearly ran straight into Papa, who was coming out of his bedroom. He yawned, stretched, and then scooped her into a hug. "Good morning, Sunshine," he said. "Or should I say good night? I forget."

"Good *night*," Nanea said with a grin. "It's a fun night, too. You're coming to the party, right, Papa?"

"Of course," he said. "The Sudas are family. I wouldn't miss Lily's birthday celebration! Just let me get showered."

Nanea sighed. More waiting! When a wet nose nudged her hand, she plopped down beside Mele, who immediately rolled onto her back. Nanea laughed. "You want a belly rub? All right. You'll give me something to do while I wait."

The next half hour felt like an eternity. Finally, Papa was ready. As they walked the short distance to Lily's house. Papa held Mom's hand and whistled all the way.

Nanea felt like whistling, too, except she hadn't

learned how. She pursed her lips together, about to give it a try.

Then she spotted something on Lily's front porch up ahead. Not something—*someone.*

Someone with black hair, a tan lanky body, and khaki shorts.

Nanea sucked in her breath just as *Mano* looked up from the porch rail he was painting. And stared right at her.

"What is he doing here?" Nanea whispered to Lily as soon as they were alone in the living room.

Lily's face darkened. "Gene was supposed to paint the porch, but he's never home. Your tutu kane told my daddy about Mano. And, well, here he is." She glanced nervously at the window, as if Mano might be listening in.

"He'd better not come inside!" said Nanea. She faced the front door as if it were the entrance to the harbor. *The Sudas are family,* she reminded herself. *I won't let him steal from them.*

Luckily, Mano stayed outside during dinner. But when it was time for cake, Aunt Betty added one more plate to the table. It was already very full, with Nanea's family, Lily's family, Tutu and Tutu Kane, and Jinx gathered around it.

"Let's invite Mano in," Aunt Betty said to Uncle Fudge.

"No!" Nanea's voice rang out louder than she'd intended. "I mean, he likes to finish his work. Remember, Tutu?"

Tutu nodded. "He's a hard worker. But he has earned a break."

Nanea's heart sank as Mano stepped inside, washed his hands, and took a seat at the table. She could feel his eyes on her as they ate cake and mochi. When Lily began to open presents in the living room, Mano stood just behind Nanea's chair.

"A sketch pad and pencils!" said Lily, opening

up her gift from her parents.

She held them out to show Nanea, who tried to smile. But all she could think about was the thief standing behind her. Was he looking around the Sudas' living room right now, deciding what to steal? Maybe he was eyeing the green Japanese vase with the delicate flowers. Or the *sensu*, the folding fan made of washi paper and bamboo.

I won't let him steal a thing, thought Nanea. *I'll watch his every move.*

That was difficult when Lily opened a paper sack and the scent of preserved fruit filled the room. Nanea's mouth watered.

"Crack seed!" said Lily, taking a deep inhale. "Is it plum?"

"Of course," said Uncle Fudge. "Your favorite. Straight from Mrs. Lin's crack seed shop. She wanted to be sure I gave it to you."

Lily offered Nanea a piece of the moist fruit.

"I want some!" said Tommy, Lily's little brother.

He held out his chubby little hands until she dropped a sticky plum into his palms.

"One is enough," said Aunt Betty. "Now that your dad works at the crack seed shop, he'll be bringing plenty more home, I'm sure!"

Uncle Fudge chuckled. "Perhaps Mrs. Lin can pay me in crack seed," he said with a wink.

Papa laughed, too. "That's right! You're working for Mrs. Lin now. Are you enjoying the work?"

"Yes," said Uncle Fudge, nodding. "It's good to be working again. But I do miss my sampan—and the money that came from a good day at sea. This job doesn't pay all the bills."

Aunt Betty laid a hand on his shoulder. "Shush now," she said. "It's time for birthday talk, not money talk."

Nanea saw a shadow pass over Lily's face at the mention of money. Was her family really struggling? Is that why Gene wanted to find work? Nanea wished there was something she could do.

She quickly handed Lily her birthday present, trying not to touch it with her sticky fingers. "Open my gift next."

When Lily unwrapped the small gray stone, she squealed. "Is it the Three Kittens?" she asked.

"Yes," said Nanea, leaning forward to show her. "I used Mary Lou's nail polish to paint the kittens on the stone. Jinx gave me the idea! He carries a good-luck charm: a river rock in his pocket. I thought you could carry this one to remind you that Donna and I are always with you—even though she seems far away."

Lily stared at the stone and then pulled Nanea into a tight hug. "I love it!" she said. "I'll carry it with me everywhere."

When Jinx pulled his rock out of his pocket and showed Lily, Nanea saw Mano eyeing it with curiosity. Would he steal that, too? Nothing seemed safe with that shark circling the room—not even a rock.

"You have one more present," said Uncle Fudge,

handing Lily a small square box. "Gene left this for you before he went to work this morning."

"Really?" said Lily. "I wish he could be here—it seems like he's never home anymore." Her eyes lit up when she opened the box and found a delicate silver necklace. "It looks like a plumeria!"

"What a beautiful gift from your brother," said Aunt Betty. "Oh, and so expensive." She showed Uncle Fudge the tag attached to the chain, and he quickly pulled out his pocketknife to remove it.

Aunt Betty helped Lily fasten the necklace around her neck. The small flower-shaped pendant sparkled against her skin.

"May I see it?" asked Nanea, leaning forward.

Lily skipped across the living room to show her. "I don't know how Gene could afford it," she said, but her cheeks flushed with pleasure.

As Lily turned to show the necklace to Jinx, Mano caught Nanea's eye. "It's easy to get something so nice," he whispered, "if one knows the right people." He was boasting again. But now he seemed to be accusing *Gene* of breaking the rules.

Like the shark god, Nanea wanted to swat that boy away with her tail. Bare her sharp teeth. Chase him out of the harbor. How dare he start rumors about Gene!

Gene is just as honest as David, she thought, remembering the letter she'd gotten from her brother. *He would never break the rules on purpose.*

While the others admired Lily's necklace, Jinx picked up the pocketknife that Uncle Fudge had left on the side table. "Is this a fishing knife?" he asked. "You mentioned that you are a fisherman."

Uncle Fudge nodded. "I was once," he said. "I hope to be again. But my knife? I carry that with me always. It was my father's."

Nanea saw Mano's eyes drift toward the knife, too, and her stomach tightened.

She pulled David's letter from her pocket, hoping to change the subject before Mano could ask to see the knife. "Lily, would you like to hear David's letter?" she asked. "It just came today!"

Lily nodded eagerly and knelt beside Nanea's chair, listening. By the time Nanea was finished reading, the room had grown quiet. Aunt Betty dabbed at her eyes, and Mom rested her head on Papa's shoulder.

"It's good to hear from your brother," said Uncle Fudge with a warm smile.

Nanea nodded. "I just wish he weren't looking forward to fighting the enemy," she said. That was the only part of the letter that bothered her—well, that and the enormous puka cut out of the middle of the page!

"I want to fight! I want to be a soldier," said Tommy, darting through the living room with his toy gun. "Pow, pow, pow!"

"That's enough, now," said Aunt Betty, pulling him onto her lap. "You're not going anywhere. You're staying home safe with me."

Nanea smiled at Tommy, but as she caught sight of Mano across the room, her heart sank like a stone in the sea.

Nothing felt safe when that boy was around. She had to find a way to keep him away from her 'ohana—for good.

chapter 9

Boys on the Beach

A-ROO! A-ROO!

Nanea opened her eyes in the darkness of her bedroom. What was Mele barking at? When she heard a familiar voice in the living room, she sprang out of bed.

"Lily! I didn't know you were coming over this morning!"

Lily was dressed, but her eyes looked tired. "I, um, wanted to talk to you about something." She cast a glance at Nanea's mom.

"Oh! Well, all right, I'll leave you girls to it then," said Mom, heading back toward the kitchen. "There'll be plenty of eggs and sausage if you're hungry, Lily."

"Thank you, Aunt May."

As soon as Mom was out of earshot, Nanea tugged Lily toward the sofa. "What is it? What happened?" she whispered.

Lily glanced toward the kitchen to make sure Nanea's mom couldn't hear her. "Daddy's pocket-knife is gone!" she whispered. "The one he showed Jinx last night. Daddy looked *everywhere* for it this morning, but he couldn't find it. Do you think . . . ?"

Nanea set her jaw. "I don't think," she said. "I *know*. Mano struck again. I knew we shouldn't have let him inside!" She started pacing back and forth, with Mele following her every step.

"Is he going to sell Daddy's knife?" asked Lily. "It's really special. It belonged to his father."

Nanea sighed. "I don't know. He *might* sell it. Unless he decides to keep it in his 'palace by the sea.'" She pictured Mano's home, filled with heaps of stolen treasure.

Then she stopped pacing and locked eyes with Lily. "Do you think we could find it?" Nanea asked.

"What?" Lily wrinkled her brow. "The knife?"

"No, Mano's home. By the beach!"

Lily chewed her lip. "I don't know. Who would take us there?"

Nanea glanced toward the kitchen and dropped her voice to a whisper. "Remember David's letter? He said you and I should spend some days at the beach. We might have to bring Mary Lou and Iris, too, but . . . I think Mom will take us. Let's ask."

As the smell of Portuguese sausage drifted out from the kitchen, Lily hesitated. When she finally nodded, Nanea saw the flash of determination in her friend's eyes.

"All right," said Nanea with a smile. "We're going to the beach. We'll get your daddy's knife back, Lily." She really hoped, for Uncle Fudge's sake, she was right.

· · ·

"You girls have some fun together today," said Mom. "Stick close to Mary Lou. And I'll be right inside the hotel if you need me."

She gave the girls a little wave. Then she strode toward the pink columns at the entrance to the Royal Hawaiian Hotel.

Nanea watched Mary Lou and Iris hurry around the side of the hotel toward the beach. "Remember what Donna always said?" she asked Lily.

Lily's mouth curved into a half smile. "Last one to the beach is a rotten egg!"

Nanea grinned. *But Donna's not here today,* she thought. *And these Two Kittens have work to do.* "Are you ready?" she asked.

Lily set her shoulders and nodded. "Ready."

As they walked around the sprawling pink hotel, Nanea couldn't believe how many servicemen they passed.

"Excuse me," she said, dodging around a cluster

of soldiers. "Pardon me," she said, veering around a particularly pale sailor. Had he just gotten off a submarine?

She knew Waikiki Beach had become a place for soldiers to rest and relax. But seeing so many of them made it *harder* for her to relax. They were a constant reminder of war.

So was the barbed-wire fence that stretched along the beach—a barrier to keep enemy ships from landing on shore. Luckily, Nanea knew where to find the puka, the hole in the fence that swimmers could duck through. David had shown her.

As she slid through the fence, the canvas bag holding her gas mask got caught. She tugged on the strap, thinking of Mano and how easily he claimed to slide under barbed-wire fences and dodge soldiers after curfew. *We're going to find that slippery boy,* she resolved, giving her bag one final yank. *We'll find him today.*

But first, she and Lily had to find a way to

dodge Mary Lou, who suddenly seemed eager to spend time with her little sister.

"Put your towels by ours," Mary Lou called to Nanea. "We haven't been here in ages. Isn't it dreamy?" She gazed out at the ocean, a smile playing at the corners of her mouth.

"The only thing dreamy around here is you," Iris teased, nudging Mary Lou with her shoulder.

Mary Lou *was* in a particularly good mood, Nanea noticed. Was she watching a handsome surfer?

Nanea checked the water. Since most of the local boys had enlisted in the Army, only a couple of surfboards dotted the waves. But none of the surfers were Mary Lou's age.

"Lily and I are going to get some shave ice," she said, placing her things in a tidy pile. "We might be gone for a while. C'mon, Lily."

"Wait!" Mary Lou called after them. "Bring me one, too, please—strawberry, in honor of my favorite sister's favorite flavor." She blew Nanea a kiss.

"Mary Lou sure is in a good mood," Lily whispered as they trudged across the sand.

"I know," Nanea said. "It's weird. She's been acting as sweet as shave ice syrup for the last couple of days."

As Nanea glanced back at her sister, wondering what was going on with her lately, something else caught her eye. She spotted two figures in the distance, walking near a clump of palm trees. One of them was a tall, thin boy wearing khaki shorts. *Mano?*

"Look!" she whispered to Lily, pointing. "There he is!"

Lily squinted. "Who is it?"

"Mano!" hissed Nanea. "Don't you see him?"

"No," said Lily. "I see two boys that *look* like him. But that's not Mano."

As the sun ducked behind a cloud, Nanea's eyes

adjusted—and she saw that Lily was right. That wasn't Mano at all! But the boys sure reminded her of him. She watched them sparring with each other, darting back and forth in the sand. Then they jogged toward the wooded end of the beach, where Nanea had celebrated her birthday just a few months ago.

"Let's follow them," she whispered, even though the boys couldn't have heard her from so far away. "I bet they know where Mano lives!"

But before she and Lily could take a single step, a voice rang out from the shave ice stand behind them. "Nanea?"

A young man in a bellhop uniform waved. It was Darrell, David's buddy. He handed a stack of towels to the man running the shave ice stand and then stepped carefully through the sand in his polished shoes.

"How's that brother of yours doing?" Darrell asked Nanea when he got closer to the girls.

She hesitated. Any other day, she'd be happy to talk with Darrell. But not today!

She looked back toward the woods where the teenage boys had been sparring. The sand was empty. *Too late,* she thought sadly. *We missed our chance.*

"David's okay, right?" asked Darrell, studying Nanea's long face.

"Yes!" she said. "Sorry. We just got a letter from him. He says to tell you hello."

Darrell smiled. "Well you tell him hello right back. And how's Gene?" he asked Lily. "I heard he left the Varsity Victory Volunteers for a job that pays the *big* bucks." He chuckled.

Nanea whirled around to face Lily. "Gene has a new job?"

Lily shook her head. "No, he's still with the VVVs. I mean, isn't he?"

Darrell looked as guilty as a dog that had chewed up something it shouldn't have. "I'm sorry,

I thought you knew. I didn't mean to spill the beans. Maybe . . . maybe I heard him wrong."

Why would Gene keep a new job a secret? Nanea wondered. Gene was as honest as his father, Uncle Fudge. He would never keep news this big a secret. There had to be a mistake.

"Where is he working, Darrell?" Lily asked.

Darrell put his hands up in the air. "I'm sorry, girls. I really don't know. Maybe you should ask Gene." When a soldier approached Darrell with a question, he seemed relieved to go.

"Lily, are you okay?" asked Nanea. Her friend looked as green as a seasick sailor. She led her away from the shave ice stand so they could talk.

"That explains why he was able to afford this," Lily said, fingering the plumeria pendant around her neck. "But if he got a job, why wouldn't he tell us? He's been looking for a job for a long time! What is he doing that he wouldn't want his family to know about?"

Nanea's mind spun with possibilities. Thanks to Mano, she could think of all sorts of secret ways a person could make money, like selling things on the black market. *But Gene isn't like Mano,* she reminded herself.

"We should just ask him about his new job when he gets home today," Nanea finally said, resting a hand on Lily's arm. "I'm sure everything's fine."

Lily nodded. But her eyes reflected the worries Nanea had darting through her mind like tiny fish in shark-infested waters.

chapter 10

The Runaway

A CREAK ON the front porch made Nanea jump. "Is that him?"

Lily peeked through the front window. "Yes! Act normal."

The girls busied themselves flipping through magazines as Gene pushed open the front door.

"Hi, Gene!" said Nanea, a little too loudly.

He ran his hand through his dark hair. "Um, hi," he said. "Is this my welcoming party?"

"It is!" said Lily, hopping up from the sofa. "Because we heard some good news today."

"Really?" said Gene. "What's that?"

As he walked toward the kitchen, Lily hurried after him. "About your new job!" she said.

Gene stopped walking.

"Darrell told us," said Nanea, trying to help Lily out. "We ran into him at the beach."

But Gene shook his head. "I don't have a new job," he said. "Darrell must have gotten his facts wrong. I'm still building things for Uncle Sam." He turned and disappeared into the kitchen.

Lily stared after him for a moment before slowly walking back toward the sofa. "Do you think he's telling the truth?" she whispered. "If he has a new job, why would he keep it a secret?"

Nanea couldn't think of a thing to say. So she slid over and made room for Lily on the sofa.

"The VVV is *volunteer* work. He's not earning any money," said Lily, trying to fit the pieces together. "Not the 'big bucks' that he told Darrell about. Not enough to buy me fancy presents!"

Nanea's eyes went to Lily's neck, but she wasn't wearing her necklace anymore—the one she had been so happy about when she first unwrapped it.

"Maybe someone loaned Gene the money

for your necklace," said Nanea. She didn't really believe it. She just wanted to make Lily feel better.

But she could tell by the look on her friend's face that she wasn't buying it.

"Should we tell your mom and dad?" Nanea asked gently. "Maybe they know something about Gene's job. Or maybe they'll know what to do."

Lily shook her head. "No!" she said, as if that were the one thing she was sure of. "Mom and Daddy have too much to worry about—with money, and the war. I don't want them to worry about Gene, too." As she sank back into the sofa, she looked very small.

Poor Lily, thought Nanea. *How can I help her?*

The next morning, after Nanea got dressed, she found Mary Lou curled up on the sofa with a book. Nanea strained to see the title: *Charm*.

She was about to poke fun at Mary Lou for

having to read a *book* to learn how to be charming. Then she realized Mary Lou wasn't reading at all. Her eyes were staring at a spot just above the pages. She was so lost in thought that she barely blinked.

What's going on with her? Nanea wondered. Her sister usually acted so grown-up and responsible. But these days, she never seemed to be paying attention. For a moment, Nanea felt as if *she* was the big sister and Mary Lou was the little one, with her head lost in the clouds.

The sound of a car pulling into the driveway brought Mary Lou out of her daydream. "It's Iris and her mom," she said. "Are you ready?"

Nanea nodded. Iris's mother was taking Iris and Mary Lou to the USO, and they were dropping Nanea off at Pono's Market on the way. "Come on, Mele," she called.

"You're bringing the dog?" Mary Lou asked, sounding irritated.

"Mom said I should," Nanea answered as she

let Mele out the front door. "She gets lonely at home by herself." Nanea wasn't any happier about it than Mary Lou. She wanted to keep Mele as far away from Mano as she could. But she didn't want her sweet dog to be lonely either.

Mele hopped right in the backseat of the car between Nanea and Mary Lou. "Don't get your dirty paws on my dress," Mary Lou scolded. "Keep her on your side, Nanea."

That sounds more like the old Mary Lou, Nanea thought, gathering Mele onto her lap.

As they drove, Nanea half-listened to Iris and Mary Lou. Iris told Mary Lou all about the letter she'd finally gotten from her brother Al. Then they went on and on about another banana-split party at the USO. But Nanea's mind was on the conversation she and Lily had had with Gene. *He's keeping a secret,* Nanea thought, *and all Mary Lou can think about is ice cream and parties!*

Nanea was surprised when Iris's mother pulled

into a parking spot in front of a tailor's shop. "I need to stop here to check on an alteration, girls," she said, grabbing her handbag. "It will just take a moment."

But Nanea didn't want to listen to any more banana talk. "Pono's Market isn't far," she said quickly. "May Mele and I walk from here?"

Iris's mother didn't look so sure.

"She knows her way," said Mary Lou. "And Mele will follow her nose to the market."

"Okay then," said Iris's mom. "Watch for traffic."

Nanea opened the car door to let Mele out. Then she waved to Mary Lou and Iris and headed for Pono's Market.

The streets were busy this afternoon, with jeeps full of soldiers and crowded buses. People filled the sidewalk, too. Nanea wished she had brought Mele's leash, but Mele was well-behaved. She barked friendly hellos to shop owners, and she only

stopped a few times to sniff curiously at a smell.
Until a truck full of soldiers drove by.

Someone whistled.

The old jalopy backfired, sounding like a
gunshot.

And Mele disappeared in a terrified flash.

"Mele!"

Nanea chased the dog down the sidewalk until
Mele disappeared in an alleyway. Nanea searched
behind the trash bins and along each staircase and
doorway, but Mele was nowhere to be found.

Just like the day Pearl Harbor was bombed, Nanea
thought. Worry swelled in her chest like the ocean
tide as she thought about Mele disappearing for
two horrible weeks.

"I *have* to find her," said Nanea, fighting back
tears. She raced toward the one place Mele might
head for shelter: Pono's Market.

She ran past Andrada's Market, past Mr. Lopez's
bakery, past the bicycle leaning against the shop

window, and straight through the front door of Pono's Market. As she pushed open the door, the bell above jingled and jangled.

"Tutu!" she cried, landing in her grandmother's arms. "Have you seen Mele?"

"No, keiki," said Tutu. "What has happened?"

"A car backfired. She ran off. I'm afraid she'll be lost again, like last time. And maybe this time we won't find her at all."

"Shh, shh . . . we'll find her. You'll see." Tutu patted Nanea's back.

"Mele ran away?" a familiar voice asked.

Nanea spun around to see Mano standing beside the cash register with Tutu Kane.

Always when I'm not here, Nanea thought. But she didn't have time to worry about Mano right now.

"I'll help," he said. He gripped the bullet hanging from his neck. "I'll use my whistle. I'll find her, I promise."

He ran out the door before Nanea could say no,

that she didn't need his help.

But the truth was, she *did*. She needed all the help she could get bringing her dog safely home!

"He can't promise he'll find her," she said out loud.

"No," said Tutu, stroking her hair. "But he will try his best."

Nanea nodded. Although Mano didn't have any regard for rules, he did seem to have a soft spot for Mele. *But if he finds her, will he bring her back?* she wondered. *Or will he steal her, like he steals so many other things?*

Through the front window, she watched uneasily as Mano hopped onto his bike. He blew his whistle as he pedaled toward Andrada's Market. Again and again, she heard the shrill sound of his whistle, until it finally faded away.

"I have to go look for her, too," Nanea said, pulling away from Tutu. "Mele needs me."

"Yes," said Tutu. "But we need you to be safe.

You'll stay in this neighborhood, okay?"

Nanea nodded reluctantly. But what if Mele had run farther away? How could she find her dog if Mele wasn't in the neighborhood anymore?

After promising Tutu she would stay close by, Nanea retraced her steps, all the way back to the tailor's shop. She hoped Iris's mother's car would still be parked out front—that Mary Lou would be there to help, or would have Mele curled up on her lap in the backseat.

But the sedan was gone. And when Nanea peered into the shop, she saw only a busy tailor and a headless dress form. No Mele.

Nanea stopped at every shop that might be a safe harbor for Mele. She asked the butcher if he had seen her dog, but he said no. She stopped at the bakery, where Mr. Lopez offered her a *malasada*. But she didn't want a sweet, puffy roll today. She wanted only her sweet dog. So she kept walking.

At the barbershop, the men in their chairs

stopped talking long enough to listen to her description of Mele. But when the barber shook his head, the men went right back to talking about the latest news. The latest battle in the Pacific. And Nanea had to turn away.

Today, she didn't care about the war. She didn't care about the black market, or whatever Mano—and maybe even Gene—were mixed up in. She only cared about finding Mele.

But her precious dog was gone—again.

chapter 11

Mango Rash

BACK AT PONO'S Market, Tutu urged Nanea
to stay busy. "Do you want to sort the penny
candy?" she asked.

Usually, that was Nanea's favorite job. So she
went to work, separating the Tootsie Rolls, lemon
drops, and chocolate kisses. She hoped it would
take her mind off Mele. But she was moving so
quickly that she accidentally dropped a few chocolate kisses into the wrong jar.

Then an awful thought struck.

I was moving too fast today. I was impatient, listen-
ing to Mary Lou in the car. If I had just waited until
Iris's mom came out of the tailor's shop, Mele would be
with me now!

The realization was almost more than Nanea

could bear. She tried again to focus on her work, slowing down to be sure she was dropping the right candies in each glass jar.

But the waiting was painful—like waiting for a teakettle to boil on the stove or for fruit to ripen on a windowsill.

When she heard the jingle of the front door and a furry face bolted through, Nanea dropped to her knees and let her tears flow.

"Mele!"

Her dog licked her tears away and wagged her bottom side to side. She whined and barked as if they had been separated for *hours*.

"I know," said Nanea, burying her face into Mele's fur. "I missed you, too, you scared, silly dog."

Then she realized that Mele hadn't come into the shop all on her own.

Mano was standing just inside the door, wearing his huge, proud smile. "She was halfway to

Diamond Head when I spotted her," he said. "She heard my whistle, and then came running for fish." As he patted his pocket, Mele barked and raced over for another treat.

"No, Mele—stay!" ordered Nanea, scared to lose the dog again.

Mano bent down to scoop up the wiggling pup in his arms. He carried Mele over to Nanea and set her down, right in the safety of Nanea's lap.

"It's okay, Momi," he said, reaching out to mess up Nanea's hair a little. "Mele is safe. She'll stay here with you."

As Mano turned to say hello to Tutu, Nanea thought her heart might burst. Suddenly, she knew why Mano's nickname for her bothered her so much.

It reminded her of David.

Mano didn't have David's movie-star smile, and Nanea knew that David would *never* break the rules the way Mano did. But when he called her Momi

and mussed her hair, it was as if David were standing right there, calling her Monkey and teasing her
in his playful way.

Mano is not David, she reminded herself as she
watched him pedal away. *Be careful.*

She felt like Mele, taken in so easily by a little
piece of fish.

But one thing was sure now. Mano didn't want
to steal Mele, as Nanea had once feared he might.
This would have been his perfect opportunity.
Instead, he had brought the lost dog home. He had
helped them both.

"So Mele returns," said Tutu with a warm smile.
"All is well."

"And was that Mano I heard?" asked Tutu Kane,
stepping out of the storage room.

"Yes," said Tutu. "He found Mele for Nanea."
She bent low to pat the dog on the head.

Tutu Kane gave Nanea a knowing look. "So
Mano did kokua for you."

Nanea nodded. Yes, Mano, the shark, had been kind—he had brought precious Mele back to her.

But that doesn't mean I was wrong about him, she thought. *Or . . . does it?*

Like sorting penny candy into jars, telling the good sharks from the bad was getting difficult, too. Yesterday, she had believed that Gene was honest and Mano was not to be trusted. Today, she knew that Gene was hiding a secret. And slippery Mano had done something kind!

Now Nanea felt more confused than ever—like Ka'ahupahau, the shark goddess, trying to protect her people.

How can I protect my family, she wondered, *when I can't even tell the good sharks from the bad?*

As Tutu began to close up the store, she asked Nanea to pack a small bag of items to bring home.

"Canned salmon," she called, as Nanea reached

for a can on the shelf. "And baking powder. And petroleum jelly. Jinx has developed mango rash."

Ouch! thought Nanea, remembering Bernice's description of mango rash. She wouldn't wish such painful blisters on anyone, especially Jinx.

"Tell him I hope he feels better soon," she said as she finished packing Tutu's things.

But later, at dinner, all Nanea could think about was that rash.

"Aren't you hungry?" asked Mom.

Nanea *had* been hungry—starving, in fact, by the time Mom put the platter of grilled 'ahi on the dinner table.

But now she could barely swallow a bite. Because she had just remembered something.

"Mom?" she asked, taking a sip of milk. "Can you really get mango rash from eating a green mango?"

Mom's forehead creased. "Some people say so. Others believe the green mangoes are the healthiest ones. But what makes you ask that, Nanea? Have you been eating green mangoes?"

Nanea shook her head. "Tutu said Jinx has mango rash." What she *didn't* say was that a green mango had gone missing from Tutu's lanai. Was Jinx the one who took it?

"Is that the sailor who does magic tricks?" asked Mary Lou. "Maybe he can just snap his fingers and make the rash disappear." She chuckled over her own joke as she reached across Nanea for the bowl of green beans.

"Mary Lou, mind your manners," Mom scolded. "I'm sorry to hear about Jinx's rash. But it'll heal. And in the meantime, Nanea, you've got green beans to eat."

As she tried to force down a few more beans, Nanea thought about Mary Lou's words. Jinx *was* pretty good at making things disappear. *He made my dime disappear,* she remembered. So was he the one who had taken the mango from the porch step?

Then she remembered her missing spade, the one from Grandmom Mitchell. She'd thought all along that Mano had taken it. But maybe she'd been wrong! Was Jinx the thief? He had been at Tutu and Tutu Kane's that afternoon.

And what about Tutu Kane's watch? Jinx was staying with Tutu and Tutu Kane. He could easily have taken the watch.

And Uncle Fudge's knife? Jinx had sure seemed interested in that knife at Lily's birthday party. *So Jinx could have taken those, too!* Nanea suddenly realized.

She set down her fork. She had lost her appetite for good now.

Mom frowned and laid the back of her hand across Nanea's forehead. "Aren't you feeling well, honey?"

Nanea wanted to tell Mom the truth. But she wasn't even sure what the truth *was* anymore. Was Mano the thief? Or was it Jinx? And why wasn't

Gene being honest about his job? Could he be mixed up in the black market, too?

Nanea had more questions than answers. Too many questions to point the finger and accuse anyone right now. "I'm just tired, I guess," she said. "May I be excused?"

"Yes," said Mom. "Maybe tonight should be a quiet night. Do you want to read or work on your flash cards? Or finish your letter to David?"

Nanea shrugged. "Maybe." She wandered to her room—David's room—and ran a finger over the spine of *The Mystery of the Brass Bound Trunk*. David had given her that Nancy Drew mystery. Then she turned toward her brother's smiling face, the one that stared out at her from the shiny photo taped to the dresser mirror. *I wish I could talk to you, David— about Jinx, and Mano, and Gene. You would know what to do.*

But Nanea couldn't talk to David. All she could do was write him a letter. And she couldn't write about her suspicions of a sailor—that would get cut out for sure!

She sighed. Censoring her words in her letters was starting to feel like lying. And she wasn't used to lying to her big brother. *If everything important gets cut out,* she realized, *why bother writing at all?*

Now David seemed farther away than ever.

When she heard music coming from Mary Lou's room, Nanea wandered to the doorway—to the room she used to share with Mary Lou. Was her sister practicing hula?

The door was cracked just a hair, enough for her to see inside. But Mary Lou wasn't doing hula. Not even close. Instead, she was dancing with an imaginary partner. Her arm was draped over some-one's shoulder; her hand clasping his hand. She hummed as she stepped side to side and then spun in a slow, graceful circle.

Since starting her job as a junior hostess at the USO, Mary Lou had seemed almost as far away as David. *She's always humming,* thought Nanea. *She barely listens to a word I say. She has this dreamy look in her eyes . . .*

Nanea sucked in her breath. She'd read a lot of detective novels, but you didn't have to be Nancy Drew to figure this one out. Mary Lou was in *love.*

Had she fallen for a soldier at the USO?

That's against the rules! Nanea remembered. Mary Lou could lose her job.

Frustration fizzed in her chest like a bubbly Kist soda. With so many important things going on right now, how could Mary Lou be so foolish?

"Nanea?" Mary Lou had spotted her reflection in the mirror. "Are you spying on me?"

Nanea didn't answer. Instead, she asked another question. "Why aren't you practicing hula?"

Mary Lou put her hand on her hip. "Because. I'm practicing for the USO dance that comes *after* our hula show on Saturday. I have to be at my best for all the soldiers who are fighting the war."

Soldiers? Or just one soldier? Nanea wondered. She wanted to ask his name, but she was pretty sure Mary Lou wouldn't tell her. *Another secret.*

Nanea marched back to her room and shut the door tight. *Why are so many people I used to trust keeping secrets?*

Trust more and judge less, Tutu Kane had said. Before the war, Nanea had trusted everyone. She had practiced the aloha spirit. But now she felt suspicious of so many people, and that didn't feel good at all.

chapter 12
Jinxed

THE NEXT AFTERNOON, Nanea was helping Lily weed her family's garden, but they were doing a whole lot more talking than weeding. "Are you sure Gene didn't drive?" asked Nanea.

Lily shook her head fiercely. "Not this morning. He got up early and walked somewhere—I saw him leave."

Nanea tried to fit the pieces together in her mind. The VVVs worked out at Schofield Barracks, past Pearl Harbor. Gene said he was still working with the VVVs, but he definitely couldn't walk that far every day. "Should we follow him?" she asked. "Tomorrow, I mean?"

Lily's jaw dropped. "You would go with me?"

Nanea nodded. She didn't have to think about it.

If Gene was hiding a secret, maybe it was because he was in trouble. Nanea wanted to help. Like Papa had said, the Sudas were family.

Lily's eyes flooded with relief. "Can you come early tomorrow? He left at seven today, so you'd have to come over before then."

"I'll be there," Nanea promised. "We'll find out where he's going, Lily." But as clouds drifted in front of the sun, she shivered. Not knowing what Gene was up to was hard, especially for Lily. *But knowing could be even harder,* thought Nanea. She felt as if she were bracing herself for a storm.

"Mom, may I go to Lily's?" Nanea called through the crack in the bathroom door.

Mom popped her head out, her hair still in curlers. "Before breakfast?"

Nanea hesitated. "I'm not all that hungry."

Mom frowned. "You know the rule," she said.

"You need to put something in your stomach. At least take some guava bread. I'll cut you a slice."

Nanea sighed. By the time she left the house with her guava bread, it was almost seven o'clock. There was no time to waste!

Outside, mynah birds chattered in the morning light. As Nanea's feet hit the sidewalk, a gecko scurried away into the dirt. She raced past a few houses. But as she neared the Sudas' house, she slowed to a walk. She veered around the side of the house, ducking behind a palm tree.

From her hiding place, she could see into the Sudas' backyard. There was Lily, sitting cross-legged by the Victory Garden! When she saw Nanea, Lily raised a finger to her lips.

Nanea silently crossed the yard. The moment she reached Lily's side, they heard the squeak of the front door opening. Loud footsteps clomped across the porch and down the steps.

"That must be Gene," whispered Lily.

The two girls raced around the side of the house. "See?" said Lily, pointing. "He's walking somewhere! Let's follow him!"

Sure enough, Gene took long, purposeful strides down the sidewalk. He knew exactly where he was going, and he wasn't wasting any time getting there.

It was hard to keep up with Gene without him noticing. Nanea ran on the balls of her bare feet, trying not to make a sound.

He walked the length of Fern Street and crossed over McCully. They followed him for another block, looking both ways before darting across Pumehana Street.

"Where is he going?" Lily whispered as she stopped to catch her breath.

"I don't know," said Nanea. "We're getting closer to Tutu and Tutu Kane's neighborhood. We're going to lose him, though. C'mon!"

As they crossed Hauoli Street, Nanea began to

wonder. *Is he going to Tutu's house? But why?*

Sure enough, Gene led them to a very familiar house. With a freshly painted white fence. And a jeep out front.

But Gene didn't go to Tutu's front door. Instead, he leaned against the jeep, waiting.

For what? Nanea wondered. *Or whom?*

When she heard voices, Nanea ducked low behind a hibiscus bush. She heard Jinx before she saw him. He was coming around the side of the garage—close enough that she could see the angry red rash on his chin. But who was he speaking with? Not Gene. Gene was too far away.

Nanea shifted her weight to peer around the bush. Through the blossoms and leaves, she saw the boy clearly. He was wearing khaki shorts. As if in a dream, she watched Jinx hand something to Mano. Something shiny and gold. Tutu Kane's watch!

She took a sharp breath, which brought Lily to her side in a heartbeat. Nanea pointed through the leaves.

Together, they watched Mano take the watch and give something to Jinx in return. A paper bag. Was it full of money?

Mano slipped the watch into his shorts pocket and took off through the backyard. Then Jinx carried the paper bag into the garage.

"Jinx just sold Tutu Kane's watch to Mano!" Nanea whispered. "And Mano will probably sell it on the black market. I can't believe it." *Jinx*, the sailor she had liked so much. The sailor she had trusted!

When Jinx came out of the garage, his hands were empty. And just like that, as if nothing had happened, he strode down the sidewalk toward the jeep, where Gene waited.

"Why is Gene going with Jinx?" whispered Lily. "I didn't know they even knew each other!"

"I didn't either," said Nanea.

There's a lot I don't know, she suddenly realized.

But if Gene was messed up in something secret, it looked as if he wasn't alone. Jinx was in on it, too. And Mano. Somehow, when bad things happened, Mano was always there.

As the jeep drove away, Nanea's eyes flickered back to her grandparents' front door. "We have to tell Tutu and Tutu Kane," she said firmly.

"No!" said Lily, shaking her head. "We'll get Gene in trouble. We have to find out what's going on first. We have to be sure."

Nanea's heart sank. She had tried so hard to keep Mano away from Pono's Market. To keep Tutu and Tutu Kane safe from his slippery ways.

But all along, a sailor had been staying with them who had secrets of his own.

Nanea's mind wandered more than once during the hula performance at the USO on Saturday. How could she tell the soldiers a hula story of peaceful

Waikiki Beach when all she could see in her mind was Jinx, handing Tutu Kane's precious watch over to Mano?

Mary Lou danced as if her mind were somewhere else, too. Her solo was the last hula of the afternoon, and often it drew the loudest applause.

But today her usually graceful steps seemed stilted. And when she stepped to the side and back again, she nearly tripped on the ruffled train of her holoku.

Even from where Nanea watched backstage, she could see that Mary Lou was struggling. Tutu could, too. Nanea heard her cluck her tongue. But Tutu couldn't stop the music and correct Mary Lou like she could during hula lessons on her lanai.

When the music ended and Mary Lou brought her hands together, reaching out over her pointed foot, Nanea breathed a sigh of relief.

There was no relief on Mary Lou's face as the thick red curtain creaked closed and she stepped offstage. She kept her eyes focused on her feet and sank down beside her *'eke hula,* the basket in which she carried her hula supplies. "I'm sorry, Tutu," she whispered.

Nanea's frustration with her sister melted into pity. She had never seen her perform so badly. And in front of so many soldiers, too! The rows of chairs in the ballroom stretched all the way to the far wall.

Tutu rested a hand on Mary Lou's shoulder. "Your mind is on other things," she said sternly. "But I see that your heart is heavy, too. Do you want to tell me why?"

Mary Lou shook her head. "No, thank you, Tutu. Not right now."

More secrets, thought Nanea. Her chest felt tight, as if she might drown in them all.

After the performance, she found Lily and Dixie ladling pink punch into small paper cups. The Honolulu Helpers were serving refreshments to the soldiers. With Mary Lou acting so strange and secretive, Nanea was happy to see her friends.

But Lily's eyes were puffy, as if she hadn't slept at all. She had worries of her own, Nanea knew.

When Lily stepped away to get more cookies for the soldiers, Dixie whispered, "What's wrong with her?"

Did Dixie know about Gene? Had Lily told her? Nanea studied her face.

No. The look in Dixie's eyes said that she was still in the dark. So Nanea couldn't share Lily's secret about Gene. *Because Lily wants to protect her family, just like I want to protect mine,* she thought sadly.

She was saved from having to explain when Dixie spilled a puddle of punch and had to run for a rag to clean it up.

After the chairs were taken away from the ballroom, a band started to play. Soldiers stepped onto the floor with junior hostesses on their arms.

There was Iris! She looked so pretty, with her

hair curled and lipstick on. But where in the world was Mary Lou?

Nanea was about to go search for her backstage. Then she spotted her sister talking with a short soldier in the corner. In her heels, she was a couple of inches taller than him. But they were laughing, and when he bowed in front of her and offered his hand, she took it.

Pretty soon Mary Lou was doing the jitterbug in the middle of the room.

"Oh, she's gotten really good!" said Lily as she came up behind Nanea.

"She has." Nanea could barely take her eyes off her sister. "Too good maybe."

"Huh?"

Nanea didn't want to add to Lily's worries, but she had to talk to *someone* about what Mary Lou was up to. "I think she has fallen in love with a soldier," she whispered in Lily's ear. "It's against junior hostess rules. She might lose her job!"

Lily's mouth opened in surprise. "Which soldier? The one she's dancing with?"

"I don't know. I'm trying to figure it out."

Nanea saw a couple of other soldiers watching Mary Lou, too. Was one of them her secret love?

"That one?" whispered Lily, pointing to a tall, thin soldier approaching Mary Lou. But when he passed her by and asked another girl to dance, she blew out her breath. "No, not that one."

As another dance began, Nanea was surprised to see Mary Lou dancing with the same soldier— again. Even though he had two left feet! When he stepped on one of hers, she threw back her head and laughed. Then she took his hands again and seemed to be showing him the right way to do it, just as she had taught Nanea in the living room.

Nanea froze. Mary Lou was sure having fun. And she seemed to be all eyes for this short, awkward soldier.

So that's the boy she's in love with! Nanea realized.

The reason why she's breaking all the rules! She nudged Lily and pointed.

"Are you sure?" whispered Lily.

Nanea shrugged. He wasn't at all what she had pictured. But as they watched her sister dance with him for another minute, Lily finally turned to Nanea and nodded.

It *was* true.

Having Lily agree made it feel very real. And very scary.

"Is she going to get in trouble?" Lily whispered.

"I don't know," said Nanea. But one thing was certain: The sister she had once trusted was definitely keeping a secret—and breaking the rules. So Lily's brother Gene wasn't the only family member they had to worry about. Now they had to worry about Mary Lou, too.

chapter 13

Operation Mele Medicine

BY THE TIME Papa dropped Nanea, Lily, and Mele off at the hospital on Sunday, Mele's tail was wagging so hard she could barely walk a straight line. It had been almost two weeks since they had last come to visit the soldiers.

And almost two weeks since we first met Mano at Pono's Market, thought Nanea. So much had happened since then! A part of her wished she could go back to that time, before all the secrets. But she could only go forward—especially with Mele tugging at her leash.

Mele led the way to the front entrance and trotted right past the nurse's station. When Nanea had first started Operation Mele Medicine, Mele wasn't even allowed inside the hospital. *I wasn't either,*

Nanea remembered. She had been too young.

But Lieutenant Gregory, a friend of David's, had found a way to get them both into the dayroom. And Mele did the rest, charming the soldiers and the staff with her sweetness and her Hula Dog moves.

"Hi, Mele," called a nurse with a starched white hat. "Are you going to dance for us today?"

Mele barked a joyful response.

"You're excited to be going to work today, aren't you?" said Nanea, reaching down to give Mele a scratch behind the ears.

Even Lily seemed cheerful as they headed toward the dayroom. Or at least she was putting on a happy face. So Nanea tried to put on a smile, too, even though she was full of worry inside.

When she saw who was waiting in the dayroom, she didn't have to pretend anymore. "Lieutenant Gregory!"

The tall redheaded officer wound his way

through the room of lounge chairs and wheelchairs to reach Nanea and Lily. "I've been looking forward to seeing you girls today," he said. "How's our Hula Dog?"

"She's good," said Nanea. "David's good, too. He sent a letter."

Just seeing Lieutenant Gregory's face made Nanea feel like maybe things would be okay. He knew David and had always looked out for him. He knew Gene, too, and had helped find him work in the spring. *If Gene is in some kind of trouble, can Lieutenant Gregory help him get out of it?* she wondered. *And can he tell me what to do about Jinx?*

Then she remembered something else. Lieutenant Gregory was the one who had introduced Jinx to Tutu and Tutu Kane! He and Jinx were friends. *So how can we talk to him about that sneaky sailor?* she wondered, her stomach clenching. *We can't.*

When Lily began playing "My Little Grass

Shack" on the phonograph, Nanea tried to smile. She called Mele's name, and the dog immediately rose to her hind legs. She danced in a pretty little circle.

All the soldiers in the room clapped and cheered for the dancing dog, and Nanea felt some of her worries melt away.

When the music ended, Nanea carried Mele to the center of the room so that the soldiers could visit with her. As Mele soaked up all the attention, Nanea took a step back. Then she sensed someone standing behind her in the doorway to the dayroom.

"May I have the next dance?" a familiar voice rang out.

Nanea whirled around. There was Jinx, his chin still covered in a red rash. *Mango rash.*

It looked painful, but Nanea didn't feel sorry for him. *It serves you right,* she thought.

"I heard from your grandparents that I might

find you here," he said. "You two put on quite a show."

But Nanea had only one question for him as she waved him out into the hall. "Did you eat one of my mangoes?"

The question popped out of her mouth before she could stop it. This wasn't a letter to David. This was a face-to-face conversation with a thief. And Nanea was done censoring her words.

Jinx gave a sheepish laugh. "I don't know if I ate one of *your* mangoes," he said. "But I did eat one from your grandparents' yard. I'd never eaten a mango before, and everyone kept saying I should try one. But . . . that might be the first *and* last mango I ever eat!"

Nanea hadn't expected him to tell the truth. But now that he was talking, she wasn't going to let him off the hook. Especially when Lily hurried out of the dayroom to stand beside her.

"Why did you give Tutu Kane's watch to

Mano?" she asked loudly, feeling stronger now that Lily was there to back her up.

Jinx looked shocked, and then his face spread into a smile. "You know about that? Well, I'm glad you asked," he said, pulling the watch out of his pocket. "Mano knew someone who could fix it. See?" He pulled on the band to show her the fixed link. "I asked him to do it as a thank-you gift for your grandpa, because he and your grandma have taken such good care of me. Your tutu knew—she was in on the secret. We're going to give it to him tonight."

Was Jinx telling the truth? Nanea glanced at Lily, who looked just as confused as she felt.

Jinx seemed so excited about doing kokua for Tutu Kane. Why would he lie about something like that? And if he had given the watch to Mano to *sell*, why would he have it back now?

"But . . . we saw him give you money for it! In the paper bag!"

Jinx laughed. "My goodness, Nanea. You have a magical imagination. Do you want to know what was in that paper bag?"

She did—more than anything.

"An old spade that Mano borrowed to start a garden of his own. It was a worn-out old tool, but he wanted to make sure to get it back to your grandfather."

Nanea's voice wobbled as she asked, "Did it have a blue handle?"

Jinx nodded. "I believe it did. It's in Mr. Pono's garage now, should you want to check for yourself."

As he slid the watch back into his pocket, Nanea leaned back against the wall. She felt like a puffer fish that had lost its puff, now that she knew the truth.

But Lily had more questions. "So where did you go with my brother Gene yesterday?" she demanded to know.

Jinx's eyes widened in surprise. "Gene Suda?"

"Yes. We saw you driving with him in the morning."

"You girls were up pretty early, then," Jinx said. "I was driving Gene to Pearl Harbor. I do it every day."

Pearl Harbor? Nanea's heart began to race again. Maybe she and Lily would *finally* get some answers.

"Why? What is Gene doing at Pearl Harbor?" Lily asked.

Jinx took off his sailor cap and scratched his head. "I don't know. Gene is pretty quiet about his work—it's something to do with fuel, I think."

Fuel? Gasoline? Nanea's stomach dropped.

"It's top secret, so I don't ask. I only drive him to the base because Lieutenant Gregory asked me to."

Nanea felt as if the wind had been knocked right out of her.

It was hard enough to believe that Gene was mixed up in something illegal. Now it sounded like Lieutenant Gregory was too!

Lily turned to Nanea with horrified eyes.

"Girls, what's going on?" asked Jinx, studying their worried faces.

Nanea waited until a few soldiers had passed by, and then she said, "I'm so confused. I can't tell the good sharks from the bad anymore."

Jinx cocked his head, the way Mele did when Nanea gave commands the dog didn't understand.

Nanea tried her best to explain. "What I mean is, there are so many rules during war about what we can say and what we can't. And everybody seems to have so many secrets. And sometimes they're so . . . heavy." She felt like Tutu's shark goddess, weighed down by barnacles in the harbor.

Lily nodded, giving Nanea an understanding smile.

As Jinx leaned against the wall beside them, he took a deep breath. "You're both carrying some pretty heavy worries for such young girls." He pulled his good-luck charm out of his pocket and stared at it for a moment. Then he began flipping the smooth rock over and over in his palm.

"I know what it's like to carry a heavy burden." He paused to clear his throat. "I carry one from the day Pearl Harbor was bombed. It's partly why I bring this rock everywhere I go."

Jinx kept his eyes on the rock as he continued. "I was supposed to be on my ship, cleaning up for inspection. But I went to the infirmary with a toothache. So I was onshore when I should have been on that ship."

Nanea held her breath, listening. Beside her, Lily had grown very still, too.

"If I hadn't gone to the infirmary," Jinx said quietly, "I would have gone down with my ship. Like all my buddies did." He paused to wipe his eyes with the back of his hand. "The truth is, I feel guilty that I survived."

Then he held up the rock. "This saved my life when the bullets hit shore. But I also carry it with me because it reminds me of all the other lives that were lost."

Nanea exhaled.

Finally, someone had told her and Lily the truth.

And she couldn't think of a single thing to say.

chapter 14

The Secret Letter

"GET OUT!"

Nanea tugged at the weed, but it wouldn't budge. When had all these weeds overtaken her garden?

She gave another tug and pulled up a tiny carrot.

Maybe nothing is what it appears to be, she thought as she tried to press the carrot back into the earth. *Nothing—and no one.*

At least she knew now that Jinx wasn't a thief. Yes, he had secrets—one painful secret that weighed him down like the rock in his pocket. But his secret wasn't what she'd thought. Jinx wasn't the thief he had appeared to be.

And Mano hadn't stolen Tutu Kane's watch

either. *But that doesn't mean he hasn't stolen other things,* she reminded herself, thinking of his lumpy canvas sack. Had he taken Uncle Fudge's fishing knife? That was still missing.

And what kind of secret work was Gene mixed up in? Jinx himself had said that Gene's new job had something to do with fuel. If he was part of the black market and selling gasoline illegally, he could get caught and thrown in jail.

Then she flashed on Lieutenant Gregory's face. He had always tried to help Gene find work. Had he gone too far and found him the *wrong* kind of work?

One thing was certain: Nanea couldn't figure it all out by herself. She needed help. She had to convince Lily to tell someone! This secret was bigger than two girls could handle.

"Good afternoon, Mrs. Lin," she heard Mr. Cruz call in his warm Portuguese accent.

"Good afternoon, Mr. Cruz."

Nanea heard the *tap, tap, tap* of Mrs. Lin's cane as she went to greet the postman out front.

Does he have a letter from David today? Nanea wondered. *Or from Donna?* She leaped up and stripped off her gloves. Then she raced through the yard toward the front of the house.

When Nanea reached the front porch, Mr. Cruz was just tucking something in the mailbox. But Mary Lou burst out the front door and beat Nanea to it.

"Just one letter today," Mr. Cruz called over his shoulder. "Maybe more tomorrow."

"Is it from David? Is it for me?" asked Nanea, following her sister back into the house.

"No. It's for me," answered Mary Lou in a sing-song voice.

"Who is it from?" asked Nanea.

But Mary Lou just smiled and ducked into her bedroom, shutting the door in Nanea's face.

A secret letter. From a secret sender. And

another locked door. *No,* thought Nanea. *Enough!*

"Mary Lou, are you in love with a soldier?" She asked the question as loudly and clearly as she had asked Jinx about the mango.

Mary Lou whipped open the door and pulled Nanea inside. "Shh! Not so loud!" she said. "Mom might hear."

Mary Lou's flushed face told a thousand truths.

"I knew it!" said Nanea. "Who is he? Is it the short soldier you danced with last night? You're going to lose your job!"

Mary Lou wrinkled her forehead in confusion. "What? You mean Arnie?" She fell back onto the bed and laughed out loud. "No! He's just a friend."

"Then who?" Nanea pictured the handsome soldiers who had been watching Mary Lou do the jitterbug. Was it one of them?

Her sister stared at her, her eyes dancing. "Promise you won't tell?" she asked.

Nanea didn't promise. She *couldn't* promise, not

if Mary Lou was breaking the rules at the USO and might lose her job.

But Mary Lou didn't wait for the promise. She told Nanea anyway. Or she showed her—the letter she had just torn open.

Nanea strained to read the messy handwriting, starting with the signature scrawled across the bottom of the letter.

"Al?" she whispered. "Iris's brother?"

Mary Lou nodded.

"You're still sweet on him?" asked Nanea.

"How could I not be?" Mary Lou slid a photograph out of her book on charm and handed it to Nanea.

The photo was creased and dog-eared—she must have been carrying it around for weeks. But even Nanea had to admit, Al looked pretty handsome in his Army uniform.

"You won't tell Mom, will you? Not yet anyway. She might think I'm too young."

Nanea shook her head. Mary Lou hadn't broken any rules. She wouldn't lose her job. This secret made Mary Lou happy and didn't *hurt* anyone.

This, Nanea decided, was the best kind of secret.

"I won't tell Mom," she promised.

But as she left her sister humming in her bedroom, there was one person Nanea couldn't *wait* to tell: Lily! Mary Lou's secret was good news—and Lily needed to hear some good news. *If only Gene's secret could turn out to be something good, too,* Nanea hoped. *If only.*

"Tommy, can you get Lily for me, please?"

He stared at Nanea with his big round eyes. "I'm guarding the door," he said. "I'm a soldier."

"I know," said Nanea. "But can you tell Lily I'm here? I need to talk to her."

Tommy didn't let her in. He closed the door,

locked it, and disappeared.

Was he coming back? Nanea tried to look through the window beside the door, but the curtains were drawn.

At least that gave her time to think. On the way to Lily's, she had wondered again: *Who can we talk to? Who can help us find out more about Gene's job so that we can keep him safe?*

The answer had come to her so suddenly, and she knew it was the right one. But would Lily agree?

Finally Lily opened the door a crack, and then widened it. "It's you," she said with a half smile. "Tommy said it was the enemy." She laughed and let Nanea inside.

It only took a couple of minutes to fill Lily in on Mary Lou's secret. But with Lily babysitting Tommy, it was hard to talk to her about Gene.

Nanea waited until Tommy had run into the other room with his toy six-shooters. Then she said,

"I know someone who can find out what Gene has been doing for Lieutenant Gregory."

Tommy poked his head back into the room. "Is Gene a soldier?" he asked.

"No!" said Lily. "Gene works for the VVVs. You know that."

Is that what grown-ups do? Nanea wondered as she stared at Tommy's innocent face. *Do they lie sometimes to keep us safe?*

She didn't want to lie to Tommy. But she and Lily had to find a way to help Gene.

"Tommy, are you still spying on us?" Lily called down the hall.

There was no answer.

"I know the perfect person to help us solve the mystery," Nanea whispered, just in case Tommy was hiding around the corner, playing enemy spy. "We should tell Mano."

"What?" Lily shook her head. "You don't even trust him. Why would you tell him?"

"Because," said Nanea. "He knows the black market. He knows the soldiers. He knows how to find things and figure things out. If Gene is involved in black market gasoline, Mano will find out."

Lily didn't look so sure.

"He'll find out, Lily," Nanea insisted. "And then maybe we can help Gene get out of it. Before . . . it's too late."

chapter 15

Playing Games

NANEA KEPT SEARCHING the sidewalk in front of Pono's Market. Now that Lily had finally agreed to ask Mano for help, Nanea wanted to talk to him right away. But would he come today?

She was hanging a "Buy War Bonds" poster in the front window when she finally saw his bicycle pull up out front. She hurried outside before he could come in.

"Momi!" he said with surprise. "You look happy to see me."

"I am," she said, not even minding that he had used his nickname for her. "I need your help." She quickly explained in a hushed voice what was going on with Gene—or at least what she suspected.

173

Mano looked proud of himself. Maybe it was because Nanea had never come to Mano for help before. Or maybe it was because she told him he was the *only* one who might know how to find Gene. Either way, he said yes, even before she was done asking the question.

"I'll help you—and your friend Lily. I'll help you, Momi." He gave her a sunny smile and a confident nod.

Nanea felt such a rush of relief, she almost hugged him.

"We can go to the beach tomorrow," he said.

"Wait, *we*?" she asked.

"Yes. You should come. I know soldiers there who'll give me information—I do favors for them all the time. But they might have questions about Gene or this Lieutenant Gregory you're telling me about. I can't answer them. You and Lily should come, too."

Nanea felt her newfound hope drain from her

chest straight down to her toes. "I can't go out after curfew," she said, shaking her head. "I'm not like you."

Mano furrowed his brow. "Who said after curfew? We can go in the afternoon. You can meet me at the beach, near my home. I'll show you my palace by the sea," he said with a twinkle in his eye. "Maybe you can even meet my brothers."

"You have brothers?"

"Yes," he said. "Lots of them."

So the mysterious Mano had a family of his own.

The next afternoon, Nanea and Lily rode their bikes to Kapiolani Park, near where Nanea had celebrated her birthday just a few months ago.

She hadn't biked to the beach since David left for basic training. Mom wouldn't let her make the two-and-a-half-mile ride without him—until today. Because Nanea said Lily *really* needed a day at the beach, which was true. And because there hadn't been anyone to drive them.

But where was Mano? He said he would meet them here!

Junker cars were scattered across the park so that enemy planes couldn't land. But the abandoned cars cast a creepy feeling over the park.

Lily must have felt it, too. "Are you sure this is the right place?" she asked.

Nanea nodded. "I think so."

When she heard voices, she rounded one of the rusted-out jalopies—and stumbled onto a group of soldiers playing cards. One of them glanced up, smoke swirling from his cigarette.

"I don't think we should be here," Lily whispered.

But then Mano was behind the girls—as if he'd stepped right out of one of those cars when he saw them show up. "Wait here," he said to Nanea and Lily.

Nanea watched with curiosity as Mano
approached the soldiers, calling them by name.
He tossed one of them a pack of cigarettes and then
squatted down beside another, talking to him in a
muffled voice.

Someone teased Mano, and he shot a joke right
back. It was like a game he played, bringing things
to the soldiers and earning their trust. And Mano
played it well.

She heard him mention Gene's name, and
Lieutenant Gregory. That's when all the soldiers
stopped talking and glanced up at Nanea. She
didn't know what that meant—or even what to
hope for.

"You're looking for Lieutenant Gregory?"
another soldier asked as he passed by the card
game.

Mano waved his hand, dismissing the question,
and the soldier walked on in the direction of the
Royal Hawaiian.

Mano got cozy, taking a seat on a flat rock. As he started telling a story, the soldiers were all ears, asking questions and cracking jokes.

It was as if Mano had forgotten all about Nanea and Lily!

"What's he doing?" asked Lily.

"I don't know," said Nanea. "Maybe he got information from them, and so he's telling one of his stories as a thank-you."

Or maybe he's just being boastful, she thought. *He likes to hear himself talk.*

Then Nanea heard another voice—one she knew well. Someone was calling her name.

As she stepped around the jalopy, she saw an officer taking long strides toward the park.

Lieutenant Gregory! Why was he here? Did he know they were asking questions about him?

Nanea fought the urge to duck back behind a car. That would be useless since he had already seen her.

So she turned to warn Mano instead. He didn't know what Lieutenant Gregory looked like, so he wouldn't know to leave and might get in trouble?

But Mano had already disappeared.

chapter 16

The Truth Comes Out

"TELL ME AGAIN why you were there," said
Lieutenant Gregory from the front seat of the jeep.

Nanea stayed silent this time. What could she
say without giving away Gene's secret?

She knew by now that Lieutenant Gregory
wasn't involved in the black market—not one bit.
He had seemed so shocked to find Lily and her
in that part of the park. And so worried. He had
picked up both bikes and led the girls to his jeep,
insisting on driving them home.

But now he wanted answers. Why had they
been there? And why had a soldier come into the
Royal Hawaiian Hotel and told him the girls had
been asking about him?

"Are you in trouble?" he asked. "Can I help?"

The question was so sincere that Nanea wanted to cry. "We need to tell him, Lily," she said, squeezing her friend's hand.

Lily nodded and took a shaky breath. "Gene's selling gasoline on the black market," she said in a rush of words and emotion.

"But only because the VVVs didn't treat him well and made him wear a black badge!" Nanea added.

"And because our family needs money since Daddy lost his fishing boat. Gene wanted to help," explained Lily.

As the truth came tumbling out, Nanea felt the weight of the world lift off her shoulders. She held her breath and waited to hear what Lieutenant Gregory would say. Could he help them? Could he help Gene?

But when Lieutenant Gregory pulled the jeep to the side of the road and turned to face the girls, he didn't look shocked. Or angry. Or worried. Not at all. He looked amused, as if Lily had just told a joke.

"Gene's not selling gasoline on the black market," he said. "I promise you. We'll talk more when we get to your house—when your parents can hear what I have to say, too."

Nanea turned to face Lily, her eyes wide. If Gene wasn't selling gasoline, then . . . what was he doing?

When Lieutenant Gregory finally pulled up in front of the Sudas' house, Nanea followed her friend into the living room and sat beside her on the sofa. There, Uncle Fudge studied them with worried eyes. "What is it?" he asked Lieutenant Gregory. "What has happened?"

Aunt Betty set out a plate of mochi and a pot of tea. But for once, no one touched her mochi. Except Tommy, who zoomed in and out of the living room like a bomber jet.

Lieutenant Gregory began to talk. "It's true that your son is no longer working for the Varsity Victory Volunteers," he said to Uncle Fudge and

Aunt Betty. "The military has asked him to do something top secret. Something important."

Aunt Betty's eyes widened, and Uncle Fudge leaned forward in his chair.

"He's building something very large, something that will take time to complete," Lieutenant Gregory explained.

A shiver of excitement ran down Nanea's spine. "Jinx said it had something to do with fuel."

Lieutenant Gregory hesitated. "I can't tell you what it is or where it's located. All I can tell you is that his work is very important, and very *legal*." He looked at Nanea and Lily when he said that. "And again, it's very much a secret. Can I count on you to keep it?"

Aunt Betty nodded and dabbed at her eyes.

"Of course, officer," said Uncle Fudge. "Of course." He was proud of Gene, Nanea could tell.

"So he wasn't lying to me," said Lily with a small smile. "When he said he was building something for Uncle Sam."

Lieutenant Gregory shook his head. "No, he wasn't lying to you."

And he wasn't breaking rules or stealing, thought Nanea. *And he's not going to get in trouble!*

But in the midst of her relief, she felt a stab of shame, too. *I doubted him,* she realized. *How could I?* She thought of the many clues that had led her to point the finger—in the wrong direction. She'd been acting like Nancy Drew. But this wasn't a made-up mystery book. This was real life.

"Now if only we could figure out what happened to Daddy's pocketknife," Lily said.

Uncle Fudge shook his head sadly. "I fear it's lost for good."

Nanea noticed the look on Tommy's face. From across the room, Lily's little brother stared at Nanea with big, worried eyes. He dropped the "hand grenade" he was carrying—a small wooden block—and stared at the floor. Did this little soldier, who loved carrying toy weapons, have something to do with Uncle Fudge's missing knife?

Nanea didn't want to point the finger again. But she *did* want to talk to Tommy. So when he sat back down and started building something out of blocks, she went to sit beside him.

"Tommy," she said, "do you have a secret? About your daddy's fishing knife?"

He didn't answer—he just stared at her with those deep brown eyes.

"I had lots of secrets, too," she told him. "But sometimes it feels good to share them. Do you want to tell me a secret?" She leaned toward him invitingly, tucking her hair behind her ear.

Still, he said nothing. He jumped up and ran away to his bedroom. When Tommy came back, he was holding something behind his back.

And Nanea knew just what it was.

...

As Lieutenant Gregory walked the girls to his jeep to get their bikes out of the back, he stopped and knelt down beside them.

"I've answered some of your questions," he said. "Now I have a question for you. Why on earth did you think Gene was involved in the black market?"

This time Lily didn't answer. She turned to Nanea, as if to say, "Your turn."

Nanea felt her cheeks burn. But now that the truth about Gene was out, she wanted to tell Lieutenant Gregory what had happened—*everything* that had happened. So she told him about Mano, the boy who lives by the beach, wears a bullet around his neck, and tells boastful stories.

"Mano sneaks under barbed-wire fences to go fishing at night. And he knows *all* about the black market, because he stays out after curfew and gets things for soldiers, things that other people can't get. He—"

Nanea suddenly realized what she was saying.

In trying to unload her own heavy secrets, had she just spilled all of *Mano's* secrets? Had she told Lieutenant Gregory about Mano breaking the law?

She clamped her mouth shut.

Gene is safe, but I just put Mano in danger.

And there was no going back now.

After Lieutenant Gregory drove away, back toward the beach, Nanea clutched Lily's hand.

"We have to warn Mano," she whispered urgently. "To tell him that Lieutenant Gregory knows about him and the black market!"

"But how?" asked Lily. "We don't even know where he lives!"

"Near the beach!" Nanea remembered. She started to climb onto her bike. Then she stopped and took a deep, steadying breath. "We should tell someone, right?"

Lily nodded slowly. "No more secrets."

Nanea sighed and gazed off toward the beach, where the sun was sinking low in the sky. That's when she saw a young man walking toward them, slowly—as if he'd just put in a long day's work.

Lily recognized him first. "Gene!" She ran to her brother and jumped into his arms.

"Whoa!" said Gene laughing. "What's all this about?"

As he set Lily back down on the sidewalk, she shook her head. "I don't even know where to start."

But Nanea did. "We have a lot to tell you," she said to Gene. Her cheeks warmed again, thinking of how hard it would be to tell him everything they had suspected of him. "But first, we need your help!"

chapter 17

Palace by the Sea

"C'MON, MELE," SAID Nanea, opening the door of Gene's jalopy so that the dog could jump inside. "Mano found you when you were lost. Can you help us find him?"

As they drove toward the beach, Gene shook his head. "So you two thought I was mixed up in the black market." He whistled through his teeth, as if he could barely believe it.

"I'm sorry!" Lily said again. "But you lied to us about your job. And you were so angry that you couldn't join the Army."

He nodded. "I know. But you have to remember this: No matter how mad I get about the way Japanese Americans are treated, I would never break the law. Got it?"

Lily nodded. "Got it."

Nanea knew in her heart it was true. Somehow, maybe, she had *always* known that Gene was honest, like his father, Uncle Fudge. Like David. But things had gotten so mixed up!

Gene glanced back at Nanea. "This Mano boy sounds like another story. If you think he's breaking the law, why do you want to help him?"

Nanea shrugged sadly. "I don't know. I just know he helped me once, when Mele ran away." She glanced down at her dog, who licked her on the nose. "And I know he needs *our* help now."

"Mano!"

As they walked along the shoreline, Nanea didn't know whether to holler Mano's name at the top of her lungs or whisper it into the wind. Was Lieutenant Gregory here, looking for Mano? If he was, Nanea, Lily, and Gene had to find Mano *first*.

"Help us," she pleaded with Mele, who trotted along the beach beside her. "Find Mano. Can't you smell his dried fish?"

Mele barked. She wanted that fish. And she wanted to help Nanea. But she didn't know how. The poor dog sat in the sand, cocked her head at Nanea, and whined.

"She doesn't know what we're looking for!" said Lily.

"Do *we* even know what we're looking for?" asked Gene, scanning the shoreline.

Nanea shook her head. Was Mano's "palace" a large building? Or a wooden shack, hidden in the woods alongshore? She had no idea!

Then she saw them—two thin boys in khaki shorts. She nudged Lily. "Are those Mano's brothers? They have to be! C'mon!" She broke into a run.

Nanea reached the boys first. "Is Mano here?" she asked. "Does he live nearby?"

Neither boy spoke. They studied her, just as

little Tommy had at the front door, trying to decide whether she was a friend or an enemy.

Then Mele barked and nosed at the taller boy's shorts pockets.

"You know what's in there, don't you?" the boy said, laughing. He pulled out a piece of dried fish and fed it to Mele.

Now Nanea knew for sure—these were Mano's brothers. And they knew she was a friend, or at least that Mele was.

When Lily and Gene caught up, Nanea introduced them to the boys. "We need to find Mano," she said again. "He needs our help."

"C'mon," said the shorter boy, waving them along the beach.

They walked so far that Nanea began to worry. Where were these boys leading her and her friends? Should she trust them so easily?

Finally, they stopped walking and pointed toward a wooded area. "You can wait inside," said the taller boy. "We'll go get Mano."

"Wait inside?" asked Lily. "Inside what?"

As Nanea stared at the woods, a structure began to take shape. Palm branches covered a log doorway, and when she ducked beneath it, she found herself in some sort of dugout.

"Nanea, wait!" Gene called. "You don't know what's in there."

It's true—she didn't. But as she stood in the dim space, her eyes began to adjust. Thatched mats covered the dirt floor, as if Mano and his brothers had been sleeping here. The walls of the cave were lined with goods, *stolen* goods: cans of pork and beans, bags of rice, boxes of crackers, a pile of oranges, and even the missing milk—the cans with the red carnation on the label.

As Gene stepped in behind her, he gave a low whistle.

Finally, here was the proof Nanea had been searching for, proof that Mano had been stealing.

But instead of feeling angry, her stomach twisted with sadness. Because she knew now that this cave was Mano's "palace by the sea."

"It looks like an air-raid shelter," whispered Lily.

Nanea nodded. "But instead of hiding in here for a few minutes during an air raid, this is where Mano has been *living* with his brothers."

Mele's friendly bark outside the cave told Nanea that Mano was here. She hurried outside to talk to him.

Mano had a string of fish on a line, and a line of boys chattering behind him. Now that Nanea could see and hear them all, she realized they weren't brothers. Not really.

One of the boys had a Portuguese accent. Two others spoke in Chinese. They were all rail-thin.

Nanea pulled Mano aside, away from the others, and warned him. "Lieutenant Gregory might come looking for you," she said. "I'm sorry—I told him too much about you, and about the things you steal and sell on the black market."

Mano cupped his ear as if he hadn't heard her right. "The black market?" he asked. The corner of his mouth twitched.

"Yes," she said. "The things you stole!" She waved her hand toward the cans, bags, and boxes of food in the cave. "You should hide them."

Mano shook his head. "I didn't steal any of that," he said. "I traded for it. I fish, and I trade the fish for food for me and my brothers. I trade at Pono's Market. Didn't you know?"

Nanea felt as if someone had splashed cold ocean water in her face.

"You trade with Tutu Kane?" asked Gene.

Mano nodded. "He knows my father, so he trusts me and knows I'm a good fisherman."

"Where is your father?" asked Lily, glancing around as if this fisherman father might suddenly appear. "Does he live here with you?"

Mano shook his head. He hung his string of fish from a branch and sat down at the base of the tree. "He's being held at Sand Island, like a prisoner," he said. "He's been there since the war started."

Gene's face darkened. "Because he's Japanese, like we are."

Mano shrugged. "Why else? And because he had a fish market that did good business. And because he is strong-headed, like me. He probably spoke out against the way he was treated."

Nanea saw something flicker across Lily's face—a memory, maybe. *Uncle Fudge had been held at Sand Island for only a few days,* remembered Nanea. *But it had felt like years—especially for Lily and Gene.*

"Where's your mother?" Nanea asked Mano. Something inside her already knew the answer.

"She died when I was little."

"Oh, Mano. I'm sorry." She sank down onto the sand beside him. "I'm sorry you're alone."

He flashed her a smile. "I'm not alone. I have

my brothers," he said, pointing to the group of boys roughhousing on the beach. "My diving brothers. We're a family—'ohana. We look out for one another."

So all Mano wants to do is take care of his family, thought Nanea. *Just like Lily. And just like me.* How could she have been so wrong about him? "I feel like the shark goddess Ka'ahupahau," she said softly. "I thought you were stealing. But you were right. I couldn't tell the good sharks from the bad."

Mano chuckled and leaned back against the tree. "No, Momi. You judged well. You didn't come here to harm me. You came here to help me." He reached out to muss up her hair, just like David would have.

"Yes, I did," Nanea said, smiling.

"C'mon, I'll show you all something." Mano stood up and waved Nanea, Lily and Gene to a spot behind his "palace."

There Nanea saw the most pathetic little Victory

Garden, with crooked rows of sandy dirt and brown, wilted plants.

"I borrowed Tutu Kane's old wooden spade," he said. "I hope he didn't miss it. What do you think of our garden?"

She shook her head and laughed—about the spade and about the sad little garden. "I think your garden needs help, Mano. But don't worry. We'll help you."

"That's right," said Lily. "We'll help you. Work is a lot more fun when you do it with friends."

Mano heard the word *friends* the way Mele heard the word *fish*. He whirled around to face Nanea and Lily. And he smiled.

chapter 18

The Way of Kokua

"THIS MEAT IS so expensive," said Nanea's customer, clucking her tongue at the prices posted above the wrapped steaks.

"We have fresh fish today," said Nanea. "It's so 'ono. May I wrap some for you?"

As Nanea led the woman toward the fish, Tutu Kane caught her eye and winked. "Go ahead and ring up your customer, too," he said, nodding toward the cash register.

Now that Nanea had memorized her times tables, Tutu Kane trusted her to handle money. He had taught her how to use the register just yesterday! She loved pressing the heavy keys and hearing the jingle of the drawer opening.

"Mahalo," Nanea said as she handed the

customer a few shiny coins. As she pushed the drawer closed, Nanea realized something. *I've learned a lot more than my times tables this summer. I've learned to trust more—not to judge others too quickly.* Tutu Kane had been right about that all along.

As she straightened out the postcards on the counter, Nanea asked him the question that had been on the tip of her tongue all day.

"Tutu Kane, is it wrong to trade food from the market for Mano's fish? Will you get in trouble with the government?"

He shook his head. "No, Nanea. It's not wrong. We're not breaking any rules. On the mainland, the government has to ration food to make sure everyone gets enough to eat. But our island—Oahu—provides more than enough for us all, if we're willing to share."

Nanea sighed. "There are so many rules now," she said. "And they're not like times tables, with one right answer."

Tutu put a hand on her shoulder. "But what is *always* the right thing to do?"

Nanea thought about that. "Kokua? Helping others?"

"Yes," said Tutu. "Very good. If you follow the way of kokua, you will never go astray."

Nanea thought of Mano, who fished at night, after curfew, to help feed his brothers. She thought of Jinx, who snuck around in the early morning to help Tutu Kane fix his broken watch. And she remembered how badly she herself had wanted to help Mano—how she had led Gene and Lily to his palace by the sea, even when she still suspected he was a thief.

Nanea nodded. She finally understood. Sometimes, when the rules were confusing, her *heart* would tell her what was right.

•••

"Do I look very handsome?" asked Tutu Kane. He sat up straight in his chair and crossed one arm over the other, showing off the shiny new strap on his gold wristwatch.

"Ae," said Tutu with a smile. "Like King Kalakaua himself."

"I thought so," said Tutu Kane. He winked at Nanea. "What a generous gift. Mahalo, Jinx."

"You're welcome." Jinx bowed his head. "It wasn't easy to surprise you, though. We have a very good detective in our midst."

He grinned at Nanea, who blushed. She wouldn't be trying to solve another mystery any time soon. She'd leave that for Nancy Drew. "I'm glad you have your wristwatch back, Tutu Kane," she said. "Now you don't have to carry that heavy watch around in your pocket."

As her grandfather got up to get his ukulele, Jinx glanced her way. "And how are your heavy burdens, Nanea? Are they feeling lighter now?"

She nodded. "Much lighter." Then Nanea remembered the story Jinx had told her at the hospital about the day of the bombing. "I wish I could make yours lighter, too," she said. She started to share an idea that had been forming in her mind, like a tiny pearl in an oyster shell. "Jinx, maybe . . ."

She stopped. Would he think she was too bold?

"What is it?" he asked. "You can tell me anything."

"Maybe you could share *your* secret, too," she said finally. "With Tutu and Tutu Kane. They would understand. And you would feel better!"

Jinx slid his river rock out of his pocket and studied it. "Maybe so," he said, flipping the rock over and over in his palm. "Maybe so. You're a smart girl."

Nanea smiled. She hoped she had helped him.

Sometimes it's not about keeping the bad sharks out, she realized now. *Sometimes it's about letting the good sharks in—in on our worries and our secrets.*

"Tutu," Nanea said as her grandmother came back into the kitchen. "Will you tell Jinx the story of the shark goddess?"

Tutu's eyes crinkled into a smile. "Maybe you should tell Jinx the story. You know it well."

So Nanea began. She told her friend Jinx all about the shark goddess who swam in the harbor, protecting the people and home that she loved.

INSIDE Nanea's World

Following new rules was a very real part of living in Hawaii during World War Two. Girls like Nanea did their best to follow those rules. For people who worked for the military, following rules sometimes meant keeping secrets—even from family members.

Gene's top secret job was based on a real military project that was constructed in Hawaii in the 1940s. Just seven miles away from downtown Honolulu, but nearly five hundred feet belowground, the Red Hill Bulk Fuel Storage Facility was being built. Few islanders had any idea that the facility existed. The men who worked on the classified project were under strict orders to not say a word about it to anyone—an order that lasted for more than fifty years!

The Red Hill facility is a series of underground tanks, tunnels, and pipelines that store and distribute fuel to Pearl Harbor and Hickam Field. Before World War Two, the Navy's entire fuel supply was stored in aboveground tanks at Pearl Harbor. The tanks were unprotected and easy targets from the air. In 1940, the U.S. government began searching for a location to build an underground storage facility. They chose a volcanic mountain ridge two miles from Pearl Harbor that was home to sugarcane fields and pineapple plantations.

Work began on December 26, 1940, nearly a year before the attack on Pearl Harbor. Crews dug long tunnels and tall shafts to support construction of twenty massive fuel tanks. The tanks were hollowed out of volcanic rock, lined with steel, and made of concrete. Each tank was as big as a twenty-story building and could hold 12.5 million gallons of fuel! Nearly four thousand people worked twenty-four hours a day, seven days a week, to finish construction as quickly as possible.

It was dangerous work. At one point in the construction process, workers had to lower themselves into the shafts by rope to insert sticks of dynamite into the rock walls. Then they raised themselves to the top of the dome and set off the explosives. Sixteen men died during construction. The project was finished in September 1943, nine months ahead of schedule. Once completed, Red Hill was bombproof and *impenetrable,* which means that no one could break into it. Thanks to people like Gene, the U.S. military's supply of fuel in the Pacific was safe.

The Red Hill facility still operates today, though it's staffed by just four members of the Navy. In 1995, Red Hill was declared a Civil Engineering Landmark, like such structures as the U.S. Capitol, the Golden Gate Bridge, the Statue of Liberty, and the Hoover Dam. Red Hill is a landmark few have ever seen, however. While islanders now know about the facility, it remains off-limits to the public.

GLOSSARY of Hawaiian Words

ae *(AYE)*—yes, agreement

'ahi *(AH-hee)*—a large tuna fish

aloha *(ah-LO-hah)*—hello, good-bye, love, compassion

'eke hula *(EH-kay HOO-la)*—a bag or basket used to carry hula implements and costumes

holoku *(ho-loh-KOO)*—a floor-length formal gown with a train

imu *(EE-moo)*—a large covered pit where food is baked by hot stones

Ka'ahupahau *(Ka-AH-hu-PAH-hau)*—a shark goddess who protected humans from other sharks in Pearl Harbor

Kahi'uka *(kah-HEE-ooh-KAH)*—Ka'ahupahau's brother, a shark god with a sharp tail

kaholo *(ka-HO-loh)*—a side-to-side movement in hula

kalua *(kah-LOO-ah)*—to bake in an underground oven

keiki *(KAY-kee)*—child

kokua *(KOH-KOO-ah)*—assistance, a good deed, to help

komo mai *(KOH-mo MY)*—a greeting of welcome

lanai *(LAH-nye)*—covered porch

lauhala *(LAH-ooh-HAH-lah)*—the leaf of the hala tree; used to make baskets and other woven items

luau *(LOO-ow)*—a party or feast that includes entertainment—often traditional Hawaiian music and hula

mahalo *(mah-HAH-loh)*—thank you

makaukau *(MAH-kow-KOW)*—ready, prepared

mano *(muh-NOH)*—shark

mele *(MEH-leh)*—song

menehune *(meh-neh-HOO-neh)*—a legendary race of small people who worked through the night

momi *(MOH-mee)*—pearl

'ohana *(oh-HAH-nah)*—family

'ono *(OH-no)*—tasty, delicious

poi *(POY)*—a starchy pudding made from pounded taro root. A *poi dog* is a mixed-breed dog, named for a now-extinct breed that was fed poi.

puka *(POO-kah)*—hole. Puka shells have holes in the center.

tutu *(TOO-too)*—grandparent, usually grandmother

tutu kane *(TOO-too KAH-nay)*—grandfather

Read more of NANEA'S stories,
available from booksellers and at *americangirl.com*

❁ *Classics* ❁
Nanea's classic series in two volumes:

Volume 1:
Growing Up with Aloha
Nanea may be the youngest in her family, but she *knows* she's ready for more responsibility. When Japan attacks Pearl Harbor and America goes to war, Nanea is faced with grown-up chores and choices.

Volume 2:
Hula for the Home Front
The war has changed everything in Nanea's world. She's trying to do her part, but it's not easy to make so many sacrifices. Hula, and a surprising dance partner, help Nanea hold on to her aloha spirit.

❁ *Journey in Time* ❁
Travel back in time—and spend a few days with Nanea!

Prints in the Sand
Step into Nanea's world of Hawaii during World War Two. Learn how to dance a hula. Help a lost dog. Work in a Victory Garden, or send secret messages for the war effort. Choose your own path through this multiple-ending story.

❀ A Sneak Peek at ❀

Growing Up
with Aloha

A Nanea Classic

Volume 1

Nanea's adventures begin in the
first volume of her classic stories.

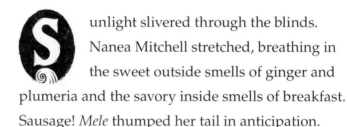unlight slivered through the blinds. Nanea Mitchell stretched, breathing in the sweet outside smells of ginger and plumeria and the savory inside smells of breakfast. Sausage! *Mele* thumped her tail in anticipation.

"Good morning, you silly *poi* dog," Nanea said, giving Mele a pat. She hopped out of bed and turned the wall calendar from October to November 1941. It was Saturday, so Nanea put on a sleeveless blouse printed with tiki huts and palm trees and a pair of white shorts.

Her fifteen-year-old sister, Mary Lou, yawned, loosening her braids as she slid out of her bed across the room. She walked to the vanity, shaking her dark waves over her shoulders, and clicked on her little Admiral radio.

"Your hair looks nice," Nanea said.

Mary Lou picked up her hairbrush and turned to Nanea. "Let me fix yours."

"It's fine!" Nanea leaped out of reach.

"Alice Nanea Mitchell!" Mary Lou scolded, using Nanea's full name. Papa had picked Alice, which was Grandmom Mitchell's name, and Mom had picked Nanea, which meant "delightful and pleasant." "Sometimes you are so childish," Mary Lou sighed.

"Not today." Nanea picked up her *'eke hula*, a basket for carrying costumes and implements. "See? I'm all ready for hula class."

While Mary Lou got dressed, Nanea made sure she had both sets of wooden dancing sticks. The *kala'au* were the size of a ruler; when she hit them together, they made a *tick-tick* sound like the big clock in her third-grade classroom. The longer *pu'ili* made a happy noise that reminded Nanea of the cash register at Pono's Market, her grandparents' store.

That reminded her of something else. "Why can't I go to work with you after class today?" she asked. "*Tutu* says I'm a big help."

"Tutu spoils you," Mary Lou answered, fluffing her hair, "because you're the baby of the family."

Nanea knew that their grandmother did *not* spoil her, and that she was *not* a baby. But before she could say anything to Mary Lou, "Chattanooga Choo-Choo" came on the radio. Mary Lou grabbed Nanea's hands and twirled her around the room, singing along with the radio.

When the song ended, Mary Lou said, "Gosh, that was fun." Her eyes sparkled.

"Hula is prettier." Nanea made the motion for swimming fish.

Tail wagging, Mele licked Nanea's hands.

Nanea laughed. "These aren't real fish, you goofy dog!"

"What's going on in here?" David asked as he ducked his head into the girls' bedroom, sending in a wave of Old Spice aftershave.

Nanea noticed the ukulele case in his hand.

"You playing today?" she asked.

Seventeen-year-old David worked as a bellboy at the Royal Hawaiian Hotel, but sometimes he filled in when one of the other musicians was sick, or surfing.

"Maybe," he said. "I'm a Boy Scout. I'm always prepared." When her big brother smiled, Nanea thought he was as handsome as any movie star. "Breakfast is ready. Come on."

The girls followed him to the kitchen.

"Good morning!" Nanea said, kissing Papa's cheek. His hair was wet from the shower.

"More like good night for me," Papa replied. He worked the graveyard shift, so he went to bed after breakfast, which was really his dinner. "Do you like my aftershave?" Papa grinned. "Instead of Old Spice, it's Old Fuel."

Nanea had heard that joke a million times, but she laughed anyway. Nothing washed away the smell of oil that Papa got from working as a

welder at the Pearl Harbor shipyard. There were
so many ships. And planes, too, at Hickam Field
next to the shipyard. David said because Pearl
Harbor was a big deal in the Pacific, Papa was a
big deal in the Pacific. That always made Papa
laugh.

Nanea turned to her mother. "Why can't I
work at Pono's Market? I'm nearly ten."

Mom tucked a lock of hair behind Nanea's ear.
"Don't be in such a hurry to grow up."

"Yeah, Monkey." David waved his fork.
"Enjoy being a kid as long as you can."

"I would love to be nine again," Mary Lou
said. "No responsibilities."

Nanea frowned. She had plenty of responsibilities! She took care of Mele and set the table
and always turned in her homework on time. But
Nanea wanted grown-up responsibilities, like
working at the market.

"Is that a storm cloud on someone's face?"

Papa teased Nanea.

She leaned her head against her father's. His hair was carrot-red and hers was black; he had blue eyes, she had hazel. The Mitchell kids were all born on Oahu like Mom. Papa had been born in Beaverton, Oregon, far away. He grew up on a farm, not in a city like Honolulu. Despite those differences, Nanea and Papa were very much alike. They loved many of the same things: the funnies, fishing, and dogs—especially Mele. Nanea wrapped her arms around Papa's neck and squeezed two times. That was their secret code for "Buddies forever."

She sat down and poured a glass of fresh pineapple juice. "Being the youngest doesn't mean I can't do grown-up things," Nanea complained. She wondered why her *'ohana*, her family, never gave her the chance to prove it.

About the Author

Like Nanea, ERIN FALLIGANT grew up
reading Nancy Drew mysteries and dancing
with her older sister to records on a record
player. Unlike Nanea, Erin was lucky enough
to grow up during a time of peace.
World War Two was a distant memory,
something she heard about in the stories
her grandparents told. She's grateful for the
sacrifices families like Nanea's made so that
others could enjoy peace and freedom. From
her home in Madison, Wisconsin, Erin has
written more than 30 books for children,
including advice books, picture books, and
contemporary fiction.